Total-E-Bound Publishing books by Natalie Dae:

Fantasies Explored
Think Kink
Thinking Kinkier

The Coterie
Lincoln's Woman

I0570491

A Gentleman's Harlot
Minute Maid

SHADOW AND DARKNESS

NATALIE DAE

Shadow and Darkness
ISBN # 978-1-78184-504-2
©Copyright Natalie Dae 2012
Cover Art by Posh Gosh ©Copyright May 2012
Interior text design by Claire Siemaszkiewicz
Total-E-Bound Publishing

Published in 2012 by Total-E-Bound Publishing, Think Tank, Ruston Way, Lincoln, LN6 7FL, United Kingdom.

SHADOW AND DARKNESS

Part One

Mistress Shadow

Chapter One

Bastinado

That attire — expensive denims, brand name polo shirt, polished leather loafers — suggests he is wealthy, but one can't always be sure from appearances. His voice, cultured, brings upper class to mind...though, again, it is foolhardy of me to assume. So often it makes an ass out of you and me.

```
Name: Luke Johnson
Preference: Bastinado
Notes: Arrogant upon arrival, which lingers at
the beginning of the session, submissive
thereafter, embarrassed upon leaving. Non-
violent. Unmarried.
```

My dungeon, one of many housed in this remodelled warehouse in London's belly, witnesses what some may say are atrocities. This black-painted room allows release of men's wants — wants they wouldn't otherwise have assuaged. It seems wives don't understand, and these men...they are, for the most part, ashamed of their desires. Society — cruel society — deems their fantasies absurd, twisted, and weird.

I do not.

The stairs outside my dungeon creak, and I wonder, not for the first time today, if it's Luke's tread. Beautiful Luke, who garners more than a second glance from the ladies.

From me.

On more than one occasion I've imagined Luke entering a bar. All heads — male and female — look his way. Women swoon at the thought of belonging to him. Men harbour secret wishes that they *were* him.

I would say Luke is well aware of the attention he commands. He enters my room once a week, always on a Monday, and the air he brings with him holds a charge. A tangible aura. I'd made a bargain with myself to keep business and pleasure separate. If I hadn't, I'd fuck him. He's one of the few clients that makes me hot...wet. One of those clients I'd break my own rule for.

Another set of creaks, heavier than the last, indicate the blond Adonis with a penchant for bastinado has arrived. Why he loves his feet caned I don't know, and I would never bring myself to ask. It isn't any of my business, although the question still burns my tongue every time I see him.

I inhale, release the breath with slow deliberation, and straighten my shoulders. Upon entrance, he'll see a black-haired woman, kohl-lined eyes steely, no-nonsense, red lips full and soft. My outfit, the one Luke prefers, resembles that of Catwoman, minus the ears. He loves the clothing, said once that he imagines the feel of it — rubbery and tacky on his hands — that stroking it while I cane him would make him come faster. I had bitten back a gentle laugh at that. He comes fast enough as it is.

He knocks on the door, and I wonder what he's been up to this weekend just past. Last Monday he'd reported his involvement in a bar brawl. The other week he'd said he'd found himself in an altercation with some man in the gym. One never has any idea of his transgressions until the session begins.

"Enter," I say.

And wait. Luke always takes a moment to turn the handle and allow himself entrance into my domain. I suspect he fights with himself as to whether he should come in. Or whether he should turn away — leave the premises, never to return. I would guess his predilection gives him sleepless nights. On the one hand he can't help what he desires, yet on the other... Maybe he thinks people would ridicule him if he let the secret out, perhaps say he was strange, off the wall. For a man like Luke, being cast out of his manly circles, scorned for his needs...well, it would crush him. He's the ultimate alpha, and alphas, at least the ones I've met, don't like slights of any kind.

The handle rattles, the keeper releases, and the door swings open. And there stands Beautiful Luke, his six-foot-six frame silhouetted by the stark hallway lighting. Blond hair, just long enough to touch his shoulders — wispy waves that call out for me to run my fingers through them, to bury my nose in their softness. Broad shoulders — so broad he almost fills the frame. A muscled chest that a woman could well imagine beneath that white T-shirt of his, one I have seen on many occasion. His nose is skewed — definitely having been broken at some point — and I like that about him. He looks rough around the edges, more than ready for a little...force in the bedroom. The thought of him switching and being the Dom whispers through my mind, and I know he's the only man I've met so far who I'd reverse roles for. To be splayed beneath him, accept everything he dishes out, looking into those blue eyes…

"Good morning, Luke." Thankfully, my voice is steady, doesn't belie the tremor racing through me just at the sight of him. I can smell him, all tangy aftershave and fresh sweat. I want that sweat on me. I want that scent so close I can't breathe.

He steps inside and closes the door, his unblemished hand with its square-ended fingers flat against the wood. He didn't fight this weekend, then. As usual, he ignores me, slaps his payment on the small wooden table beside the door, and stalks past, heading for the changing room at the back. Inside, he turns to snap the red curtain across for privacy, and his gaze meets mine, a hint of disgust in those heavenly irises. He holds me in contempt, I know. However, I don't care—much. He arrives, he pays, he gains what he seeks, and leaves.

Leaves me longing for next Monday.

I play a game every time he arrives. Will he preserve his arrogance upon leaving the changing room this week? Will he ignore the myriad instruments hanging on the walls instead of emerging to hang his head and take in the tools one by one from beneath lowered lashes? To check if anything new has gained a place on one of the hooks? I'm amused as to why he bothers. His only interest so far has been the riding crop.

His naked emergence today matches every other.

I sigh inwardly. No change makes Luke a very dull boy. But still sexy as fuck.

He wrings his large hands, positioned over his flaccid penis, and brushes his wrists against his golden pubic hair, creating an almost inaudible rustle. He flicks his gaze from the instruments on the wall to the leather table in the centre of the room and then to me.

I nod.

He lies on the bed.

So the session begins, and I prepare myself to ask the same questions as every other Monday.

I stand at the base of the bed, legs akimbo, red-polished, long-fingernailed hands upon hips. I stare at him to ensure our roles are in place. His gaze doesn't meet mine for more than a second. He gawps at the ceiling, blinking, blinking...

"Do you want nasty talk, Luke?"

"Yes, Mistress."

I narrow my eyes. Oh, how he pushes my buttons, flouts the rules at the start. "Mistress what?"

He blinks again, rapid-fire fast. "Mistress Shadow. Sorry, so sorry, Mistress Shadow."

Gone is the scorn he entered with. He appears frightened of me now — the man he tells me he usually is far out of reach. No bunched fists ready to fight, no mouth ready to shoot off — just a pliant customer reduced to uncertainty, rigid on the bed there with his eyes darting left to right.

"That's better. Do you want music, fucker?"

His hands flutter beside him upon the leather, and his sweaty palms leave a wet patch for an instant before the warm air devours it. He nods, overly eager.

"What music do you want?"

"Pink," he whispers. "Pink, Mistress Shadow."

I flare my nostrils, pretending I don't think about how he always has to have things the same. Perhaps it's his way of maintaining control while outwardly giving it up to me.

"The same as last week, you predictable shit?"

Tears fill his eyes, yet he nods again, smiles. Why the tears? I've always wondered that about him. Is he battling with himself, angry that he needs this?

Annoyed that he has to come here in secret to have his desires met—the one thing he craves, given by a woman he knows nothing about. A woman he pays. Such a shame he can't find a partner of like mind.

Me, for instance. If only he'd ask, send out feelers to see if I'm interested. Of course, I wouldn't jump at the chance right away. I'd make him think I needed time to ponder what he'd offered, but in the end I'd accept.

It would make my life.

My stilettos click-clack on the tiled floor. The stereo, positioned on the stainless-steel table to our right, nestles between the Tupperware boxes containing butt plugs, nipple grips, small paddles, handcuffs. Luke's breathing labours—a staccato of exhalations—and I know without turning around what's happened. I jab the 'Forward' button, select track six, press 'Play'. The opening bars of Pink's latest song shimmies out of the speakers—low, just loud enough to hear.

I turn to face Luke.

His impressive erection bounces, reaching just an inch below his blond-haired belly button. My, my, if I didn't work here... Yes, he would fill me nicely, and that head—that divine, swollen, pre-cum-glistened head—would feel smooth, so smooth against my tongue.

My mouth waters.

I swallow. "And do you want me to cane your feet, imbecile?"

My heart rate soars, a surge of adrenaline infusing my body, akin to a swift shot of whisky on an empty stomach. Head giddy, I stare at him staring at the ceiling.

"Look at me, boy."

He complies, jaw tightening, his eyes burning me with hate...hate for his predilection, hate that I'm the one who administers his punishment, hate that he can't help himself, can't be any other way. And he's tried — tried to deny it — but it rules him.

"Why don't you embrace your desires, accept them as a part of you and enjoy? Why do you insist on hating me and loving me at the same time?"

"I-I don't know, Mistress."

"Mistress *what*?"

He widens his eyes, his penis bobs erratically, and the veins on his neck throb. He lifts one hand from the bed, hovers it over his cock. Oh, how he aches to palm it and bring himself off. The indecision is written all over his face.

He slaps his hand against his thigh — once, twice — and squeezes the muscle on that beautiful, sexy leg. "Mistress Shadow. Please, hurry...hurry."

I stalk to the left wall and glare at him as I walk. "Are you telling me what to do, fuck-wit? Are you?" Riding crop now in hand, I swish it before me, its harshness indicated by the swoosh of displaced air. "You know how that displeases me. How the crop will bite your feet harder." I test the crop against my leather-gloved palm and resume my position at the bottom of the bed.

Luke stares at the ceiling again, at the red up-lighter emitting a soft, almost ethereal glow. He slips his hand from his thigh, moving his fingers to pluck at the cowhide, and his cock strains, the vein pulsing, pulsing.

"Answer me, damn it!"

The crop whips the leather beside his leg, and he jumps and worries his bottom lip between perfect white teeth.

"No, Mistress Shadow. I'm not telling you what to do. Honestly. I wouldn't... couldn't —"

"Then shut the fuck up and do as I tell you. Lift your legs. Feet into the stirrups. Is that tight enough on your ankles?"

He shakes his head.

"Tighter?"

Nods. Smiles—his eyes tear-filled once more.

"Then let us begin."

I lean forward and press the button that lowers the stirrups. Martin, my last client, had requested a butt-plug fuck, hence the previous stirrup height. Now, Luke's feet hang level with my waist, the perfect position to cane his smooth size twelves, to whip the pads of his pretty toes.

"Have you been a good boy this week, Luke?" I ask because I'm curious. Each week he tells me a little more about himself, and I've built up a picture of his life. Where he goes, what he does, just in case I decide to… To what? Follow him? I shake the thought away.

"No, Mistress Shadow."

I stand to the side, my back facing the instrument-riddled wall, and raise my arm. Graceful, such a graceful movement. The cane arcs through the air, slaps against his insteps. Luke's toes curl, and he brings his knees up, stirrup chains rattling with his sharp movement. A pleasure-pain yowl erupts from his mouth, and he pants, smacks his hands onto the bed, fingers twitching to grab his cock and masturbate.

He's predictable. The session won't last the hour.

My breath hitches, and I close my mouth, breathe through nostrils made wide by desire—desire that pools in my belly. With the next strike, my clit throbs. Wetness seeps into my panties. God, how I want this man to fill me...but only because he's so pretty, his body so perfect, his personality one that draws me.

Anger at the cruel trick of fate, at the prod from the devil urging me to renege on my own promise, I snarl, "What have you done to be bad, ugly boy? Hmmm? What have you done since you last visited me?"

Luke straightens his legs, prepares for the next hit. He wiggles his toes, lays his fingers against the bed — still, so still. The rise and fall of his chest lessens from its previous rapidity, and he opens his mouth to speak.

"I had three one-night stands, Mistress Shadow."

I gasp — as I always do at this point — though Luke isn't to know my exhalation isn't part of the session. I want to be those women. Even one night with him would be enough. Or would it?

"Three? Why, you filthy, dirty little bastard!"

Crack!

His yelp bursts through smiling lips, his teeth luminous in the semi-darkness. Again his fingers try and fail to grip the leather beside him, again his knees draw up, revealing the base of his perfect arse. And I wonder what it would be like to fuck that sweet, puckered hole with a dildo. What it would be like to hear him groan in pleasure. Alas, Beautiful Luke has no such desire — that I know of — for such an act, so my musings remain just that.

My panties receive another layer of moisture.

Fuck. Fuck!

A deep inhalation ensures my professional head sits upon my shoulders and that my business-like demeanour comes to the fore. Time for self-gratification when he leaves.

Luke adopts his relaxed position. Eyes closed, he awaits the next strike. His refusal of a blindfold during his first visit told me that although he closes his eyes for each lash, he can't be that ashamed, not really. He could look as I raise the cane and swat his soles, but the anticipation of when that swat will be, of his ears picking up the delicious swish as the cane journeys towards him, proves more pleasurable than the actual contact of crop on skin.

"I'm sorry. So sorry, Mistress Shadow. I won't do it again. I won't have meaningless sex again."

I smile, just a slight lift of my lips, and ready myself for the final administration. Luke never makes it further than four strikes.

"I should think not!" I say, my voice making me sound disgusted, angry. "Let us hope that your inability to walk in comfort after this session is a reminder of your sins. Filthy boy. Dirty, unclean, useless boy."

Crack!

Knees up, toes clenched, right hand off the leather and on his cock...pumping, pumping...his foreskin stretched, bunched, stretched, bunched...three, four, five times. Luke grunts, wails in both disappointment and triumph, his hand movements faster, faster still. His ejaculation spurts in a juddering, creamy arc and lands on his sunshine-yellow chest hairs.

Wet, so wet, I stifle the urge to massage his cum into that delightful, alluring chest. To lick it from my fingers, savour the taste. To position myself above him and entice his cock back to life, to fill me, to make me come.

The crop handle receives my ire, and I squeeze it in my fist. My breasts ache, throb to be handled, to have my nipples pinched by those square-ended fingers that now stroke his deflating cock.

He opens his eyes. Looks at me. And blushes with such ferocity I fancy his cheeks itch. All business now, I release his ankles and reach beneath the bed for the small sachet of wet wipes. I hand them to him, and he takes them in his clean left hand. Eye contact, though brief, assures me that yes, he still hates me and what I represent.

Turning, I walk to the left wall and hang the crop. The small table beside the door beckons, and, on autopilot, I step to it and pick up my payment. Two hundred pounds. Fifty for Madam, one hundred and fifty for me.

A door, butted against the corner of the right-hand wall, at the other end to the client's changing room, calls for me to walk through it without a backwards glance. But I don't. I never do with Luke. And, as always, before I step inside my changing room to indulge in five minutes of the lonely pleasure that Luke's visits incite, I hope to catch a glimpse of him before he enters the changing room. One more sight of him before the next client arrives. After all, a week between sessions is a long time. Too long.

And, as always, he stands in the curtained doorway, face aflame, tears in his eyes, and mouths, *"Thank you."*

Chapter Two

He Knows

I live with Mistress Darkness—real name Klara—in a top-floor flat not far from the warehouse. I share my space with her...my thoughts too, when my musings about Luke get too much and I need the sound advice she can give me. She's a nymphomaniac, literally, hence her fucking most of her clients. She can't help herself.

Tonight I'm restless, in need of going out. These walls are driving me crazy, cooping me up, the air seeming stagnant from the flat being closed up all day. I want new sights, new air.

I want Luke.

I can't deny it any longer. I thought I could remain professional, and for many months I have, but that man... God, he's driving me insane. The look he gave me earlier today was different somehow to the usual last glance. It was as though he wanted to tell me something, more than the thank you he'd muttered. Did he want to tell me that for all the months he's been visiting me, he wants to take it to the next level?

That was just my wishful thinking, wasn't it?

After arriving home, I strip and shower, wash my hair then step out and dry myself softly. I imagine

Luke moves the towel between my legs and over my breasts, that he stoops to take a nipple into his sweet mouth and suckle. I wish my thoughts so true that it hurts to think of him any longer. Nothing I can do will erase the burn inside me — nothing except going to find him.

I dress in jeans, a tight-fitting black T-shirt, and training shoes — the kind of clothing that won't look out of place at the gym. Yes, I'm going, will enter that building as a woman who has a mind to keep fit and toned, all the while looking for the man who haunts my thoughts more than any man should.

Ready, with gym shorts and another T-shirt in my sports bag, I scribble a note for Klara. She'll be disappointed I'm not here when she arrives home. She has demons to deal with, needs someone to talk to — I appreciate that — and if my need for sex with Luke tonight is anything to go by, I pity her that she has to cope with this for the better part of her days.

I take the lift down to the ground floor of our building and make my way across the lobby. These flats are top end — apartments really, and cost a fortune to rent — but with the money we both make, it isn't a strain on our finances. The lobby looks like someone's living room — dark red leather sofas and chairs, a few tall plants dotted about, and plush cream curtains hanging at the windows. The security guy sits behind a desk, lifts one hand as I breeze past, totally unaware of my mission tonight and the fact that my stomach is in knots. What if Luke isn't there? What if I caned his feet too harshly today and he can't work out?

What if he *is* there?

I confess I haven't thought this through properly. I decided on a whim to do this, to try and become a part of his life—the one he tells me snippets about, the one I've always longed to be in. What if he doesn't find me attractive? I can hardly waltz in there with his favourite Catwoman outfit on so he knows it's me. He's never seen my face, won't have the faintest idea of who I am. Perhaps that's what I need. For Luke to get to know me as the real person I am and not what I do for a living. Oh, there's no doubt that I love my job and what I do seeps into the bedroom, but there's a whole other side of me he has no clue about. How I love the smell of roses—the feel of their petals, so soft, like the head of a man's cock. How I like to use the Jacuzzi just off the lobby of our flat and close my eyes as the bubbles tickle my cunt, wishing Luke's tongue did the tickling. Too many things to mention, too much information about me, that I want him to learn.

Outside, I breathe in the fresh air and head for my car, a trusty little light blue Ford Escort that sounds as though it's choking when I bring it to life. I've had it since I first passed my test and can't bear to part with it. It hardly gives off the impression of the lifestyle my clients suppose I lead, but once I leave that warehouse, I'm me—Ursula Meadows—a woman who wants what I assume most others do. A man who loves me unconditionally, warts and all, who doesn't mind that I don't look perfect every minute of the day. A man who accepts that I'm human, not some pretty little doll to be paraded around on his arm. I've had my fair share of men like that, and I hated it.

My car indeed barks out a vibrant cough but after a few revs admits defeat in trying to make out it's dying. I swerve out of the parking area and take the road towards work. Funny how the gym Luke uses is a couple of warehouses down from the dungeons. I wonder if he thinks of me when he returns this way on a Monday night, or whether he just thinks of what I do for him.

I park and secure the car, my stomach clenching along with my cunt. I so want him to be here, need him to be here, and if he isn't, I'll be devastated. Now that I've taken this step, if it doesn't go to plan, I'm not sure when I'll have the courage to repeat it.

Please let him be here.

I enter the gym, shocked to see one of my clients behind the desk. A beefy black-haired man who enjoys having his arse whipped with a crop as thick as a butt-plug. He widens his eyes as I approach the desk, and a deep blush fills his cheeks. A lock of his fringe covers one brown eye, and he shakes his head to move it. I feign nonchalance and pay for my session, him taking the cash in a shaking hand. He mutters something about the changing rooms being to the left, but I'm already walking away, eager to see if Luke's working out.

Quickly, I change and stow my bag in a locker. With nerves jangling, I push through the door leading to the gym and take a minute to look around. Men outweigh women by five to one, muscles pumped by various pieces of equipment. Sweat drips from them, patches of it darkening their T-shirts, even though air conditioning keeps the place cool and fresh. I scan them all, searching for that blond head, suddenly frantic that I won't find him.

It feels as though I'm invisible—cocooned in a bubble, watching, them oblivious to my presence. A creepy feeling of being the only person on the planet occurs, similar to a time when it had snowed calf deep and no one except me seemed to have ventured outside. Yes, they are there, but they're all busy, thoughts on their own troubles, not interested in me.

What if, when Luke sees me, that dark scowl of his appears? What if he'll be angry I'm here, encroaching on his private life, bringing his fantasy world out into the open? Do I have the right to force things, to manipulate them just because I've fallen in love with him?

I tense further, imagining many facial expressions from him, all negative. And really, this excursion may be for nothing, this anxiety for nothing. He may not even be here.

Relief pours into me at the sight of him on a running machine, hair wet from exertion, sweat glistening on his upper arms. His white vest top showcases his tanned shoulders perfectly, and I'm nearly undone. I want to rush over there and touch him—run my hands over his wet skin and kiss him senseless. I want to feel his lips on mine, have him probe my mouth with his tongue, his hands gripping my hair. Shaking my head a little, I ignore the images rushing through my mind and calmly walk towards the running machines as if I come here every night. I have my own at home, so I'm not worried about making a fool of myself, but running beside Luke might take some getting used to.

There's a spare machine next to him, and I stand on it, switch it on as though he isn't beside me, and begin to run. I'd forgotten to tie my hair back, and I wonder if he recognises it. That's a stupid thought, isn't it? Long black hair is long black hair. Any number of women could have the same style. I stare ahead, seeing him in my peripheral vision, pleased to note he keeps glancing my way. I think of the one-night stands he's mentioned. Even though he'd said earlier he wouldn't have meaningless sex again, I don't believe him. If I offered it, he wouldn't turn me away...unless I wasn't his type. Or would he?

The burning desire to know these kinds of things, to know him intimately, sharing secrets and showing one another who we really are, has me running faster. Adrenaline surges through me, fuelling my need to appear a gym bunny who knows what she's all about. I want to exude confidence, be a woman who catches his eye.

He slows, lowering the runner speed until he's at a complete stop. Stepping off the machine, he comes to stand in front of mine, and for a moment I'm unsure what to do. I wasn't expecting this, and I stumble slightly, cursing myself a blue streak. He tilts his head, studying me intently, and an awful thought springs to mind.

Has he recognised me? My eyes? My hair? My hands?

He steps back in full-appraisal mode now, unabashed that I'm aware of his scrutiny. I stare into his eyes, remember how they'd filled with tears, and see that he has the ability to mask both sides of himself very well. If he can do it, so can I.

I smile, keeping up my pace, and wait to see what he'll do next.

"Do you want to go for a drink after?" he asks.

Startled by his offer, I switch the runner off and brace myself against the front. I catch my breath, looking at him with what I hope comes across as surprise. And I am surprised. I hadn't expected it to be this easy. Then the nasty, ugly thought that he does this all the time snaked through my mind, souring my happiness.

I glance at my watch. "I could do. It'll have to wait at least half an hour, though. I've only just got here."

"That's fine. I need to use the weights yet."

He strolls off without a backwards glance, and I watch the sway of his arse, the true swell of it hidden beneath his baggy grey joggers. If only he knew I'd seen him naked, knew who I really am, he might not be walking with such an assured stride.

The next half hour almost kills me. I run and run, never looking his way, unable to in case he spots me watching. I don't want him to think he's got me in the bag. He needs a large dose of reality, to see that not every woman faints at the sight of him and gives him what he wants. I hold back a laugh.

Who am I kidding?

* * * *

The Peddler's is a thriving pub a few streets from the gym. I sometimes have lunch there, giving myself a break from the dungeon and all it entails. After showering, and with immense relief that the half hour was up, I'd met Luke in the car park and suggested where we go for that drink.

I stand in the pub doorway and seek him out. He sits with his back to me at the bar, having driven here faster than me, his mid-blue denims and dark red T-shirt making the colour of his hair stand out. It's still slightly wet from his shower, and damp patches pepper his collar. I walk towards him, soaking in the fact that I'm here, out of work hours, with him.

I stifle the urge to pinch myself and sit on the vacant stool next to him, pulse thrumming and a squirm of nerves in my belly. "Hi."

"Hi. What are you drinking?"

I note his pint of lager and smile. Dutch courage, or something he indulges in after his gym sessions? "Just a Coke, please."

He raises his eyebrows. "Diet?"

"No, normal, thanks."

He smiles, turns from me to order, then gives me his full attention after. "I haven't seen you at the gym before. You go often?"

"Not really. I usually run on my machine at home." I belatedly realise he might recognise my voice. Shit. I can't change it now. "I fancied a change tonight. Something…drew me to the gym."

"Oh, right. Something…or someone?"

He quirks a brow, sardonic smile on his lips, although it doesn't appear one of spite. More that he's got my measure. The prickle of a hot blush on its way itches deep beneath my skin, and I hope to God it doesn't bloom. Does he know who I am? I can't tell, and not knowing makes me feel unsure of what to do next. Should I drink up, thank him, and leave? Have I made a massive mistake doing this?

I plunge in with the truth. "Someone."

"Ah." He lifts his glass to his lips and takes a sip. "Did you find them?"

"Him."

"What's your name?" he asks.

"Mist—Ursula."

"Mist Ursula? Interesting."

He regards me with a piercing gaze, a light smile on his face as he lowers his glass without looking where it lands on the bar.

He knows. Shit, he damn well knows. No, he can't do. Stop thinking like that.

"I'm Luke."

"Lovely name." God, I sound so banal, so insipid. He's really not going to go for me. I've messed up. Shouldn't have done this. Should have just left things as they were. What if he doesn't come to the dungeon on Monday now? What if I never see him again after tonight?

What the hell have I done?

"Listen," he says. "You look nervous as hell. How do you feel about me doing some talking? I'll tell you a bit about myself, and then if you feel comfortable, you can tell me something about you."

He was smooth, I'd give him that. Nothing like the stuttering man he became when I whipped his feet. Does that mean he's ashamed of what he desires? I resist the urge to blurt out that I love a man—him— who knows what he wants and goes out to get it. But that won't serve any purpose other than to perhaps make me sound desperate, odd...a bunny boiler. And I'm the opposite of Mistress Shadow tonight—just a woman with natural feelings of anxiety when out on a first date. I'd thought I could maintain my work and bedroom roles, I'd be a witty, charming, in-control-of-herself date that he wouldn't forget. Instead, he's saddled himself with what he must think is an inexperienced girl. And I am just that, really. I dream a lot—pretend that I'm exactly like Shadow, this woman unencumbered by nerves, who always knows the right thing to say at the right time. A woman similar to Luke, who knows what she wants and isn't afraid to reach out and grab it, even if she *does* display the inward rattle of her nerves outside her body.

And mine are showing—my hands shake and I'm sure fear of this going wrong must be showing on my face in the form of a worried expression. Yes, I'm doing that now by being here—going for what I want, I mean—but it took me a long time to gather my wits and take myself out of my comfort zone and into his other world.

Here...now.

As he talks about himself, I watch his mouth, how his lips move with each word. He mentions work—an auditor of all things...I didn't expect that—and how going to the gym every Monday night isn't the only time that day he visits the warehouses. I freeze, search his face for signs that he's clocked me, but there's nothing there except pink-tinted cheeks and sad eyes.

With a sudden turn in conversation, he says, "I wish I could find someone who... It doesn't matter."

I sit more upright, lean towards him and touch his wrist. The heat from him wings through me, and I swallow to try and stop my throat from drying out. "No, go on. Please. Someone who what?"

He shakes his head, the flush on his cheeks deeper now, and lifts his glass with a hand that matches mine—unsteady. He sips, staring at the optics behind the bar, and my heart goes out to him. He wants to tell me about himself, his true self, I know it, but he's wondering if he's taking a big risk. Especially if he doesn't suspect who I am.

He puts his glass down but doesn't look my way. "There's this woman. I go to see her on a Monday. She's... Shit, I shouldn't be saying this."

"It's okay. I don't mind."

"Look, I'm going to come right out and say it. I fuck around a lot, yeah? Looking for someone like her but never finding her. That sounds so fucking cheesy, doesn't it? I want her, and part of me wonders whether I just want her because she understands what I need. That... Shit, I've never spoken about this before, but I have to, got to tell you. I want all of her, to know what she's really like outside of the situation we're in on a Monday. But she..."

He looks at me, and I'm so damn confused. Does he know I'm me or not?

"But she what?"

"She's out of my league, knows what I'm like. She won't want me, some guy who fucks around, gets into fights. And even though she does what she does, I don't see her as that kind of person. She's not dirty or cheap. She's... Fuck, she's beautiful."

God. He's talking about me. Me!

He takes a gulp of lager then bashes the glass down on the counter. "Listen, I have to go. I shouldn't have asked you to come here...should have just left you alone, left things how they were."

He stands and walks to the door before I have a chance to stop him. Scrabbling off my stool, I follow him out into the night. My mind is full of *he knows, he knows, he knows* and I have no clue how the hell to make this right. If he doesn't visit me again... I can't bear to think about it.

"Wait!" I'm frantic not to let him go, not to have things left like this.

He stops beneath a lamppost in the parking lot, the amber light rendering his hair orange. He turns, glances at me sideways, and my heart goes out to him once more.

"I always wondered what you were really called," he says, shoving his hands into his jeans pockets.

I open my mouth but nothing comes out.

"Your ring," he says, nodding to my hand. "Gave you away."

Automatically, I glance down at my hand, the large diamond of the stand-out-and-scream-it's-expensive variety glistening on my middle finger. *Fuck.* I look back up. He smiles sadly, as if taking all of me in because it's the last time he'll set eyes on me. Then he walks away.

And stupidly, so stupidly, I let him.

Chapter Three

Trussed

The fear of the unknown is a mysterious thing, for our imaginations conjure many a scenario and inflate them beyond their initial origin. What starts as a new client with a desire for being trussed brings forth the word that sounds the same – trust. I'm always amazed at the level of faith these men bestow upon us...dominant strangers.

```
Name: David Shanks
Preference: Trussing
Notes: New client. Though polite on the
telephone, he sounded impatient, angry even.
Madam has been alerted that the panic button may
go off. Requested balls and penis trussing and
for the rubber nurse's outfit. Booked an hour-
long session.
```

Mr Shanks' earlier telephone call caught me in between clients. His request for a visit today caused alarm—not borne of fear, but rather that I had to scan my mental diary and work out who else was due to visit today.

I had two free hours before Mr Delirious and Mr Grouchy.

The black leather nurse's outfit, popular among the men who prefer enemas and foreskin sutures, rarely makes an appearance otherwise. In my experience, those who desire trussing aren't fussy about my attire. Their minds are…elsewhere, their eyes usually shielded with blindfolds or PVC masks.

I shrug, adjust my black hold-ups, step out of my changing room, and into my black-walled dungeon. I press '*Play*' on the stereo, and the softness of Haydn fills the room. Humming to keep my mind occupied on my job and not Luke, I hunker down to one of the steel drawer sets below the table and open the top drawer. Inside, various shoelaces of different lengths and thicknesses lay in packets. A green spaghetti lace catches my attention, and I place it on the table ready for Mr Shanks' arrival.

Muffled moans filter through the adjoining wall. Mistress Darkness uses the room next door. She was already in bed by the time I arrived home last night then gone this morning before I had the chance to speak with her. I take it that she's upset but there isn't much I can do about it now.

The telltale creak on the stairs outside my room raises the hairs on my neck, as is usual with a new client. I never know what they'll be like. A voice on the telephone can only relate so much. He'd sounded a little irked. It's possible that he may never have done this before and his fear of the unknown sparked a gruff conversation. No matter. All will soon be revealed.

A brash knock, and the dungeon door swings open without his awaiting my command for him to enter.

He'll suffer for that.

His appearance is nothing like I'd envisioned. In my mind, this man had possessed a height and build similar to Beautiful Luke, except his hair shone blue-black and a beard of stubble smattered his square jaw, his dimpled chin. This man who stands with hands in suit trouser pockets, trousers with hems that bunch against his shoes, the matching jacket too long on the sleeves, reminds me of Bob Hoskins.

His bold, brown eyes appraise me from my nurse's hat to my peep-toe, black stiletto shoes, his mouth a tight, impatient line. I form my lips in a replica of his and hold back derisive laughter. One mustn't be too dominant in the first few seconds.

"Good afternoon, Mr Shanks. My name is Mistress Shadow. Your payment must go on the small table beside the door before any activity takes place."

He closes the door with an elbow, the resulting slam a blood-sucking leech on my skin. "You can call me David." He slaps a brown envelope on the table and lets loose a huff of air.

Yes, definitely an angry man.

I wonder for a second whether his demeanour will change when he's naked and on the table. Time will tell. Part of me doesn't relish the next fifty five minutes — if he lasts that long — yet the perverse side of me looks forward to tying his bollocks just a little too tightly.

"Thank you. David, you may undress in the changing room back there" — I point — "and once undressed, you can lie on the bed. Do you have any other preferences you would like to explore today other than those we discussed?"

The label inside my dress tickles the base of my back, and I resist the urge to scratch.

"No." He sighs. "Like I said on the phone, just trussing." He stalks past me, his mumbled "Bloody women never listen!" like a splash of bleach on an open scab.

Bastard.

He snaps the changing room curtain across the doorway, closing off further conversation. Many of my regulars welcome chit-chat at this point, but this man clearly doesn't require my vocal calming.

I don't want to speak to him anyway. I wish it was yesterday, that Luke was the one getting changed. I wish it was next week already and Luke had just walked through that door.

He may never come here again.

I close off the painful thoughts and think of Mr Shanks. I suspect his tune will change within the next few minutes. Men like him tend to have inflated egos while clothed, yet the moment the garments come off, revealing a less-than-perfect body, their attitude alters.

His re-entry to the room further smashes my assumption. He struts proudly to the leather bed, and although his weight produces a loud creak, he settles down unperturbed.

Odd little man.

"Chop-chop," he says.

Hands upon hips, I stare at him, walk towards the end of the bed, and adopt my dominant pose. I've been told that my eyes can reduce even the strongest man into obedience, and Mr Shanks is no exception. He can't meet my gaze for longer than fifteen seconds.

Satisfied our positions are established, I ask, "Blindfold, David?"

He grunts. "Please, Mistress Shadow."

Ah, so he knows the drill, then.

His penis stiffens a little, and his podgy hands slap at his member to prevent a full hard-on.

"Good work, David. I prefer to truss a soft cock."

His face breaks into a smile—such a contrast to his previously stoic expression—and his cheeks redden. "Thank you, Mistress Shadow."

I take deliberate steps towards the steel table and select a black satin blindfold from one of the tubs. I lay it over David's eyes and, as he lifts his head, I snap the elastic strap into place. He lets loose a quiet groan and resumes his previous position.

I waste a few moments unwrapping the lace from its packet. The plastic rustles, the sound an overly loud accompaniment to Haydn and David's sharp intakes of breath in the background. I hold the lace up and drop it into my palm. It pools, reminiscent of a wiggly garden worm.

Back at the bed, I stand to David's left side. "Do you require just the balls, or is a tied head also to your satisfaction?"

He nods, his action bordering on maniacal. A whiff of his underarms assails me, as does the aroma of his lower region. I muse on whether he washed in a disinfectant-based soap—the scent a heady mixture of TCP, lemon, and something I can't quite fathom. Cinnamon, maybe?

He smiles, parts his legs, and I lift his testicles, thread the lace beneath them, and bring a short amount up on the other side. With assured grace from much practice, I begin tying a knot, pulling the lace as tight as I dare while watching his face for signs of discomfort. It seems he experiences none—or none he wishes to admit—for his lips remain slack and smooth. As the top of his sac is puckered either side of the lace, I deem him sufficiently tied and move on to his cock. Using the long, free end of the lace, I wind it around the head of his penis, leaving two inches of slack between his balls and dick. His hard-on, when it finally arrives, will pull on the lace. Unable to point north, his erection, straining against the lace, will, so other clients have told me, bring almost unbearable pleasure-pain.

"You may become erect now, David."

His cream-toothed smile widens.

"Are you sure there isn't anything else I can do for you? Name-calling? The paddle? A whip?"

David blushes. "Please, Mistress Shadow. I-I would like you to..." He strokes his penis, his swollen balls. "I-I..."

The hard side of me thaws a little. Perhaps his recent comment about women never listening belongs with his other personality. I step away from the bed and walk to the wall that houses my dominatrix's repertoire.

"I can peg your penis if you wish, David. I have been known to administer fifty pegs to a man's cock and balls."

"Nuh...nuh!" David rubs his palm against his cock, and it hardens, pulls against the restraints.

"Or I can administer electric shocks if you prefer. Ones that sting beyond your present comprehension. Would you like that?" I tap my foot, letting him know my impatience. Such an act brings forth his need to be dominated, and he licks his lips, clears his throat.

"Uh. Ugh."

"David! Answer me properly!" I yell and smile at his chin dropping to his chest.

"I-I want...want you to flick me with a rubber band."

"Flick you? Flick you where, David? Your arm? Your leg?" I step closer to the bed and lean down, my mouth beside his ear. "Or your big, fat cock?"

He nods. "Yes! Yes, Mistress Shadow. My cock. Oh, yes please."

I stride to the other side of the room and yank open the drawer beneath the one housing the laces. "Thick or thin, David?"

"T-t-thin. Hurts more, Mistress Shadow."

"Indeed it does." I study him, gauge his reaction to my next words and decide he'd welcome some nasty talk. "You're a filthy little pervert, aren't you, David?"

He palms his cock harder, the fingers of his other hand twisting his engorged testicles. "Yes, Mistress Shadow. A dirty pervert. Yes."

"Dirty perverts need to be punished, don't they, David?"

"Y-yes."

His backside leaves the bed and slaps back down again several times in his excitement. Such a contrast to his earlier behaviour. I had begun to think this session would be a disaster. Not so now that I've found his weakness.

"Shift down to the bottom of the bed, filthy boy."

He scoots, his underside squeaking against the leather, until the backs of his knees meet the bed's edge. "Is that far enough, Mistress Shadow?"

"It is. Good boy. Now, lift your legs."

He does so, toes splayed in his ecstasy, and I grab his ankles then roughly shove his feet into the stirrups.

"I'll get a fabulous shot now, David. Is that what you want? A fabulous shot? A stinging, ball-numbing flick or two?"

He slaps at his reddened penis and grunts, licks his lips again. "Uh, uhm, ahh, more. More than two, Mistress Shadow."

"Ah. Not only are you a pervert, a filthy boy, you're also greedy, David. I don't like greed. Therefore, I'm going to flick you harder."

He gyrates to such a degree I ponder on whether the session will be over before I get the chance to administer his wishes. At least Luke held off for a time. I imagine the blond beauty on the bed instead of Shanks, hoping it'll help me through this session. This is my job, I have to do this today, but hell…I really don't feel like it. I want to go home and wallow, wish things had gone differently last night. But I can't. Anger at that burns my gullet, and I know I'll take it out on Shanks.

"David! Leave it alone. Do you want to come before you get your ultimate pleasure?"

His hand whips away from his cock, and he places both palms on the bed beside him. "I-I won't touch it again. I-I promise, Mistress Shadow."

I flare my nostrils, though not from desire as I do with Beautiful Luke. "Don't make promises you can't keep, little boy. We both know you'll paw at yourself after the first flick."

"I won't! I promise I won't, Mistress."

I smile. "We'll see."

Kneeling down, I hold the rubber band between the pointer finger and thumb of each hand and stretch it taut. My mind wanders back to the beginning of the session. To his rude entrance. To the fact that he's here and Luke isn't. The head of his penis points towards me, trussed as it is, its colour that of sloes. With the band held four inches from his bulging privates, I let go of one end. It snaps against the tip of his cock. David yelps, releases a hiss between clenched teeth, and immediately grabs the tip, his fingers grasping, prodding, wrenching.

"More. More, Mistress."

"*What?*"

"Please. Please."

"Mistress what?"

"Shadow. Mistress Shadow."

"That's better."

I flick again. And again. "You lied to me, pervert, when you said you only wanted trussing. And you implied I didn't listen to your initial telephone request. Had I been another type of woman, your hurtful words could have cut me to the quick." *Flick!* "However, you're a liar, aren't you, because you agreed to a blindfold and requested a rubber band." *Flick!* "Will you lie to me again, David?" *Flick!* "Will you? Will you?"

Flick!

Hand still pawing, he writhes on the bed, his lips pulled back, the movement of his legs jostling the stirrup chains.

"Answer me!" I shout.

"No, no, I won't lie to you again. I'm sorry...so sorry, Mistress Shadow."

"Apology accepted, but should you lie to me again, I will refuse to entertain you in the future. I hope I've made myself clear?"

"Yes!"

"Good." I pause. "More flicking, David?"

He groans, nods.

"Harder, David?"

I gain the same response, pull the band as far as it will go without snapping, and move closer to his scrotum.

And release.

His gasp, pursued by an animalistic yell, drowns Haydn. His cock vein undulates, and I stand so as not to be hit by his ejaculation. Pre-cum glistens, and the first spurt of sperm smacks the edge of the bed with force. The second and third ejections follow, drip down the bed and splatter on the floor.

David—the liar, the hypocrite—relaxes, his feet swaying in the stirrups. I hand him tissues and wet wipes. He holds them in a hand as limp as his cock, his breathing harsh.

Latex gloves on, scissors in hand, I say, "You may wish to keep the blindfold on while I cut the lace. Some men find it…difficult to watch."

Job complete, I collect my payment, walk to my changing room door, and lean against the doorjamb. Without turning around, I say, "You may leave the table and get dressed now, Mr Shanks. Your session is over."

"Thank you. Thank you, Mistress Shadow."

The squeak and shuffle of him leaving the bed invites my lips to smile. "Will you be back, Mr Shanks? Perhaps last longer next time? You've paid for an hour and not used up all your time."

His feet slap against the tiled floor. "Yes. Yes, I will."

"Without the attitude next time? The lies?"

"Yes. Certainly. So sorry, Mistress."

"And it's Mistress *Shadow*, not just Mistress. Remember that."

"Apologies, Mistress Shadow."

No reply necessary, I smile wider, enter my changing room, and close the door.

Chapter Four

Calling

My smile vanishes the moment I'm alone. I should have called in sick, because that's how I feel. Groggy, unable to get into role properly, my mind on whether Luke will return next week now we've met outside of the dungeon. I'd found it difficult to sleep last night, his words floating through my head until they twisted and turned into a tornado of mixed messages that ended up making no sense at all. My stomach churns. I want to throw up. I can't leave things like this. I have to make them right again, have to see him again.

With an hour and a half before Mr Delirious arrives, I make a snap decision—one that could get me into a lot of trouble. But love—or is it obsession?—does strange things to a girl, and before I can stop myself, I walk out of my dungeon clutching Mr Shanks' money as though I'm making an early deposit to Madam's safe. That's my excuse if I get caught.

Downstairs, I walk through the foyer where several men sit waiting on pine ladder-back chairs set in a row in front of the large windows that face onto the customer car park outside. Some stare at the wide desk opposite, where Shelley—our uber-sexy, blonde daytime receptionist—is busy filing her perfect long nails.

I see Mr Delirious has already arrived. God, he's an eager one. He glances up from reading a porno magazine where he sits in the far corner, catches my eye, and smiles a secret smile. He's never seen me in a nurse's outfit before and widens his eyes, nodding approval. I wonder if he'll ask me to change out of my usual outfit I wear for him, back into this one. Whatever. I'll do whatever it takes to get through this God-awful day.

Shelley doesn't look up as I walk behind the desk and enter Madam's office. Madam isn't there, probably out shopping for more tools of our trade or those high-heeled shoes she's so fond of wearing. Thanking my lucky stars, I put the cash on her desk, ready to pick it up if Shelley decides to come in and talk to me.

Madam is old-fashioned in that she keeps records of our customers in files and rolodexes. I quickly scan through the small box holding white cards that have contact numbers on them, my heart beating wildly at doing something so forbidden. It's a shame there aren't any addresses, but a phone number will do.

I find what I need, write it down on my palm, put the money in the safe, and enter the information in Madam's daily earnings book. Hopefully I did this fast enough that Shelley won't ask questions. I take a deep breath, curling my hand so she can't see the number but not tight enough that the ink will smudge. I step out of the office, note Shelley is busy booking another customer in, and give Mr Delirious a coy glance before disappearing back to my dungeon.

Locking the door, I hurry to my private room and settle on the beanbag bed. I shuffle about in my handbag, feeling for my phone. I'm not meant to use it while at work, but this is one call I have to make. With butterflies going crazy in my stomach, I flatten my hand and recite the numbers, pressing the corresponding buttons on my keypad. It's now or never. I have no time to dally about. In an hour, Mr Delirious will knock on the door and if I don't make this call now I'll have another couple of hours before I can.

I press the '*Call*' button. Lift the phone to my ear.

He answers after four rings. "Hello?"

My breath catches in my throat, and I push myself off the beanbag, standing there knowing seconds of silence have passed and I could fuck this whole thing up again by not speaking.

"Hello?" he repeats, voice impatient. "Look, if you're one of those wankers who like giving dirty phone calls, just fuck off, yeah?"

"No, I'm not." There. I've spoken, and God, I feel sick again.

"Mistress Shadow?"

"Yes, it's me, Ursula."

"Shit. Fuck. Uh, um, how did you get my number?" He doesn't sound worried, more curious than anything. A shuffle sounds, as though he's getting up or walking around.

"Does it matter?" *Please say it doesn't.*

"No, I just...I wasn't expecting—"

"I want to see you again. Try going out for that drink again. Would you want that?" I babble, splurging it out in a rush before I can stop myself saying it. He's going to think I'm an utter geek. "It doesn't matter if you don't. I understand. It might be difficult, what with you coming here and—"

"You're calling from the warehouse?"

"I am."

"Is that allowed?"

"I don't care that it isn't."

"Shit. Does that mean…? Do you…? Fuck, you make me nervous. *This* is making me nervous."

I take a deep breath and decide to open up like he'd tried to do in The Peddler's. "What you said last night. I've been feeling the same way. Mondays…well, they're the highlight of my week. I wish every customer was you. I pretend they are. That sounds creepy, doesn't it?"

"No, no it doesn't. I know what you're trying to say. I just…I never thought… What with me telling you the shit I get up to every week, I didn't think you'd be interested, but at the same time I thought I should be honest. Christ, I don't even know whether you're allowed to date customers. Are you?"

"I'm not really meant to, but you don't have to be a customer to get what you need."

Did I really just say that as Ursula, or is Shadow orchestrating how I behave because I'm here, dressed up, in the dominant zone?

I have no time to ponder that further. His breathing fills my ear. I close my eyes and listen to it, imagining he's beside me. That we've just had sex and those breaths of his are from how frantically we've fucked. Wouldn't that be something? To hear that? To know him fucking me caused that? Or to know that me riding him—Luke holding my tits in his large hands, stroking the nipples with his thumbs—made him so breathless he feared never being able to suck in a lungful of air again?

My heart speeds up and I grow wet.

He says nothing, and I'm too afraid to speak in case it breaks whatever spell we've got going here. Is he imagining too? There's something happening, I can feel it—a buzz of excitement that I'd swear crackles down the phone line.

"Christ," he says again. "Um, how long you do have to talk?"

I open my eyes and look at the clock on the wall. "I have an hour before my next client." It feels weird saying that, knowing Luke knows what I get up to during my work day. He'd said it didn't bother him, but if our roles were reversed it would kill me to imagine him with other women. Those he sleeps with, I put out of my mind, pretend they don't exist. If I didn't, I'd burn up with jealousy.

Does he have to do the same?

"Can you get out?" he asks.

"Get out?"

"To meet me. Are you allowed to use that hour for a personal break?"

"Yes." *Is he going to ask what I think he is?*

"I work ten minutes away. I can slip out. I want to…I need to see you."

Oh my God. "I can do that." I hope I sounded calm, not the eager, excited girl I feel inside. "I'll change into my next outfit then meet you out the back. I have a light blue Ford Escort. An old one. I'll wait in it."

"Okay. See you then."

He cuts the call, and I stare at my phone, unable to process what just happened. I'm meeting Beautiful Luke outside in my car, at his request. I'll be seeing him again. The thought of it brings tears to my eyes, and I blink them away at the same time as slipping my phone back into my bag. I strip out of the nurse's uniform, place it on a hanger, and hook it on the rail that stretches across one side of the room. Taking the Catwoman outfit, one Mr Delirious also requests, I pour myself into it, thinking it poignant that I'll be meeting Luke wearing what he loves. With a quick glance in the mirror, I fix the face mask in place and take a deep breath. My nerves are on fire, legs a little weak, and my stomach somersaults several times in quick succession. I breathe out slowly, will myself not to panic, grab up my car keys, then leave my private room.

After checking the dungeon is ready for Mr Delirious' arrival, I unlock the door, lock it again once I'm on the landing, then almost fly downstairs. I have wings, the earlier fogginess in my head gone now, and round the newel post with as much grace as I can considering the state I'm in. I glance at Mr Delirious, who gives me another secret smile while looking me up and down. He winks. I smile in return, then speed down the hallway between the stairs and Shelley's desk to the back door.

Outside, I take another calming breath of the cool day's air and look around the staff car park. A car I don't recognise is parked beside mine, and I wonder whether we have a new girl on the books or if Luke has arrived already. I have no clue what he drives, but the sleek black Peugeot isn't a machine I'd imagine him buying. No one is sitting inside it, so I get into mine and glance at the rear view mirror more times than I care to admit. It isn't healthy to look every other second, is it?

He'll be here. I hope…

I rest my head on the steering wheel, sucking in a deep breath to calm myself the hell down. Who would have thought a man could reduce me to this? Me…a woman who has the appearance and mannerisms of one in control of absolutely everything? I wonder what Luke would think if he knew I was on the verge of becoming so out of control to be unrecognisable as the woman he knows? It's something I want him to find out, if he sticks around long enough.

If things work out the way we both seem to want.

I stare at my shoes resting on the pedals, and think about how my life has changed since last night. I'd had no idea how Luke felt—I'd actually imagined he hated me, for God's sake—so to hear him say he's thought about me in the same way I think about him is a little...shocking.

As is my passenger door swinging open and the man himself getting inside my car.

Beautiful Luke is sitting beside me. In my car. Looking at me. Smiling.

"Hi," he says, out of breath. "I got here as fast as I could."

I swallow, return his smile, and imagine I look all kinds of geek just staring at him the way I am. I can't help it. He's so bloody gorgeous. So...not someone I thought would be interested in me.

"You okay?" he asks, a frown threatening to crease his brow.

"Yes," I manage, my face heating beneath the mask. "It's just...odd to see you here in my car."

"Oh." He glances down at his hands, laces his fingers together and circles one thumb around the other.

"Not odd in a bad way, nothing like that. Surreal, that's what I meant."

"Oh, right. I see." He looks up at me. "Take the mask off? *That's* odd, seeing you wearing it when we're not...in there." He jerks his head in the direction of the dungeons.

Gladly, I pull the mask away, then wonder if my make-up has smudged from my face being hot. It's too late to do anything about it now, but I bite my bottom lip all the same and wait for his reaction to tell me I look awful.

"You're so very beautiful," he says, untangling one hand and lifting it to my face.

He cups my cheek, strokes the skin beneath my eye with his thumb, and I'm all kinds of messed up now. I want to laugh and cry. I want to raise my hand and cover his. I want to cup *his* face and stroke *his* skin. So why don't I?

Because I can't move. Because I'm so frozen by the fact this is actually happening that I can't do anything but stare at him. I have so much to say and no courage to say it. I have so much love to give this man and may well lose the opportunity to do so because I'm such a quivering wreck.

I rustle up a smile and hope that'll suffice as an answer.

"It's different here, isn't it?" he says.

I nod, thankful my answer didn't need words.

"And I've thought about this," he continues, "for the longest time. Ever since I first visited you. Mad, right?"

Smiling again, I grab some courage and touch his cheek with two fingertips, drawing them down then along his jawline. There's the slightest hint of stubble, and the rasp of it on my skin travels through my fingers and straight to my cunt. He pulls my head towards him, our noses nearly touching. His warm breath, scented by mints or chewing gum perhaps, fans my face...and God, I want him to kiss me.

"Am I talking too much?" He looks worried. "Because you're not saying anything and I keep wanting to fill the silence and—"

I press my lips to his, the barest touch. My heart patters wildly, and for a second I lose the ability to breathe. His lips feel so hot, so smooth, and I add a little more pressure, tentative to push my luck in case he recoils. In case he's changed his mind, even though he said what he said and —

He takes the lead and crushes our lips together, and oh, the good Lord above blessed me on this day. With my stomach bunching, my whole body shaking, I open my mouth and let his tongue slip inside. The heat of it seeps into mine, and I close my eyes, let him explore while I do the same, wondering if this is really happening or whether I've fallen asleep on my beanbag and will wake when my next customer knocks on the door. It's like...like the very first time, when the initial flush of love grips hard and I can think of nothing except the man I'm kissing and how he makes me feel. He lifts his other hand and slides it into my hair, holding my head steady as he deepens the kiss. I reach out with my free hand and touch his thigh, all the while wondering if I should. Nerves rattling, I stroke his leg, go a little too far upwards and brush his crotch with my thumb.

He's hard, the side of his erection beneath my touch, and I almost spring back in alarm. I hadn't expected that. I just thought... I don't know what I thought.

Luke eases our kiss into soft pecks, and I open my eyes to find him watching me.

He pulls back, mouth still very close to mine. "Better than in my dreams."

I don't know what to say to that. A lump of emotion fills my throat and tears sting the backs of my eyes. The last thing I want to do is start bawling, so I force myself to answer.

"Same." One word, but it will have to do. I can't manage any more than that. I'm breathing too hard, too fast, and my heart... It needs to stop beating so erratically.

"Do you...will you...I mean, can I see you again?" He stares at me with eyes half-closed and so damn dreamy.

"Tonight?" I whisper.

"I can't tonight. An audit. I have to get it finished by tomorrow."

"Ah."

"But I might get it done earlier than I thought. Would after eleven be too late? I need to see you again. I can't...not."

I know exactly how he feels. "After eleven's fine." *Any time's fine.* "I'll give you my number."

"I saved it after you called."

"I saved yours, too."

If I watched this on TV, I'd think it was the cheesiest thing going, but here, right now, it's the most beautiful conversation I've ever had. Luke can talk about pig's trotters or the average rainfall in Wisconsin for all I care. Just hearing his voice, feeling his breath as he speaks, is enough to make me want to close my eyes and drown in him forever.

Cheesy. Adorable. Wonderful.

"So I'll ring you, then?" he asks, hand still in my hair, thumb still stroking my cheek.

"You will," I say, fingers still against his jaw, thumb still brushing his cock.

"When do you finish in there?"

"Sixish. It might be sooner if... It doesn't feel right talking about my job."

"It's fine. I don't mind. You're different here, with me. You're not Mistress Shadow now."

"I could be. If you wanted." *But I don't think I'd pull it off very well. Not when you're holding me like this. When your mouth is so close to mine I just have to nudge forward a bit and kiss you again.*

"Maybe another time. I like Ursula at the moment."

He moves closer, kisses me again, and all sense leaves me. I don't care about the time, what day it is, that we're both playing hooky. I don't even care if I get caught and lose my job. That's how much I want to be here.

I don't want to be anywhere but here.

Luke draws back again, lowers his hand from my hair and glances at his watch.

I know what's coming.

"I have to go."

"I should, too."

"I don't want to."

"Me neither."

It's like the stuffing has been knocked out of me. My body seems to weigh nothing, and all I have inside me is a fluttering heart and lungs struggling to take in enough air.

"One more kiss?" he asks. "Please?"

And my mind joins that stuffing, disappearing so all that remains of me is a longing to seek out his tongue and have him kiss me into oblivion.

Chapter Five

Flagellation

A client once asked, "Why do you do this?"
I replied, "Because I do."
Life sometimes takes us down unexpected paths, and what once seemed abhorrent becomes...tolerable. I derive satisfaction from certain aspects of my work, flagellation being one of them — especially when a certain someone joins in the fun.

```
Name: Simon Whittle
Preference: Flagellation
Notes: Also known as Mr Delirious, Simon Whittle
displays over-the-top reactions to the whip.
Though he appears distressed at times, he assures
me it is all part of the play.
```

Mr Delirious is due to arrive shortly, which allows me enough time to calm down from my mad dash back into the building. I try to compose myself, but hell, all I can think about is Luke, his touch, those kisses.

I pinch myself. It hurts. I smile.

I want to sing and dance, to whirl around the dungeon, arms outstretched, my hair flying. I want to tell the world Luke kissed me, he really kissed me, and that he'll be ringing me later to let me know what time we can meet up. I left the car park a breathless wreck, watched him walk away backwards as though he didn't want to turn his back on me until he absolutely had to. Wasn't that the loveliest thing?

I still can't believe this is happening to me.

And so it's inevitable that annoyance builds inside me at the thought of having to entertain Mr Delirious, that neither myself nor Luke can drop the rest of our day's work and take off somewhere, anyplace but where we currently are.

Too hot, I unzip my catsuit, opening the fronts to allow the air to cool my torso and breasts. I take a bottle of water from the small fridge in my private room and sip slowly, feeling the liquid travel down into my stomach. After a quick look at the clock, I sigh and put the water back inside the fridge.

Time to get to work.

But I don't want to.

I'm going to take my frustrations out on Simon Whittle. He knows I do this – we've discussed it – and he's a party to my need to vent. 'The harsher the better,' he'd once said. 'Make me bleed,' he also said.

To look at him, you'd figure him a bank manager, a headmaster, or an insurance salesman. His career is far from any of those. A suit denotes many jobs, yet his doesn't require one. He chooses to wear them because it gives him a semblance of control in his uncontrollable life. Odd then that his penchant is for a whip to leave bloody welts on his backside. He's hardly in control of that.

No, his wants go deeper, back to childhood, but if I thought about his life – the story of which told to me while we shared a table at Jarad's and sipped cocktails one evening—I wouldn't be able to perform his desires.

The musky smell of arousal from the last time I donned this outfit wafts to my nostrils as I re-zip the suit from pubic bone to neck. Memories of Luke invade my mind again, of how he makes me so wet, horny, needy…

However, instead of the Catwoman mask, today I must pander to Mr Delirious' requirements. I tug a gimp mask over my head and face, peer through the eye slits, breathe through the mouth slot, and smell through the two small nose holes. My long hair, caught in the neck of the catsuit, itches my back. My client prefers it tucked away in this fashion. It bugs me, but I'll do anything for one hundred and fifty pounds.

Anything?

No, not sex. Unless Beautiful Luke offers.

In the last five minutes before Mr Delirious arrives, I buckle my thigh-high stiletto boots, don black leather gloves, and rush from my changing room into the dungeon proper. Simon has an aversion to lying on the leather bed without his customary plastic sheet. Something about the *crinkle-rustle-crinkle* of it as he squirms heightens his enjoyment. I stare at the range of whips hanging on the wall and ponder the fact that my client provides his own. Maybe he has a special attachment to it. Its appearance is less than pleasing. The leather straps are old, worn, and no matter how hard I scrub them afterwards while he's in the changing room, the bloodstains remain.

The familiar creak of the stairs pulls me from my thoughts, and I cock my head, waiting to see if the client strolls past and into the dungeon two doors down. A soft, almost inaudible knock sounds on my door, and I position myself at the end of the bed, legs apart, bottom just resting on the cowhide.

I don't want to do this today.

"Enter!" I fold my arms beneath my breasts.

The handle wrenches down, and Simon Whittle bustles in, a maniacal smile on his thin, clean-shaven face. His suit trousers, creases pressed into their fronts, look sharp enough to cut skin. How incongruous he must seem behind the counter weighing out fruit and vegetables. I suspect the other employees protect their casual clothing with an apron and laugh at this diminutive, fox-like man.

"Mistress Shadow! Oh, how I wished it would be you today. And it is, yes, it is. Do you know how happy that makes me? May I hug you before we begin?"

Without waiting for my consent, he gusts forward and envelops me in his spindly arms. A heady scent slaps me, a combination of Joop! and toothpaste. I think of him so recently looking at porn and wonder if that's why he's so worked up. So excited.

"Now, I must get undressed, yes? Do you have a plastic sheet? And here, here's my whip. Oh, and my payment." The carrier bag he takes it from flutters noisily, and he shudders with what I assume is anticipation.

He asks the same questions every time I see him. Mr Delirious almost skips past me to the back of the room. I place the money and whip on the steel table to my right and retrieve the sheet, snap it out of its folds, and lay it on the bed. I glance up. He enters the changing room, turns, poses to close the curtain, and winks.

"Won't be a tic!" he says, and a giddy laugh erupts, blending into the symphony of the curtain rings against the metal rail.

I pick up the whip and pace the room, slapping the straps against my palm. A smile touches my lips at thoughts of how he'll change once he emerges, naked and vulnerable. Though he's said he puts on an act, a part of me wonders if he's telling the whole truth. His whistled tune echoes through the dungeon — *Imagine* by John Lennon if I'm not mistaken — and I inhale a deep breath to ready myself for what's to come.

The tinkle of the curtain rings, and then, "Mistress Shadow? Please may I get on the bed?"

The game has begun.

"Yes, bad boy. And if you ruck up the sheet, I'll whip you so hard — do you understand?"

His flaccid cock springs to attention — a surprisingly large erection for such a slim fellow. "Yes...yes, I understand." He nods and shuffles over to the bed, lying down with deliberate care.

"I can hear the sheet rustling, cocksucker."

He grabs his penis, yanks it a few times, his eyes beseeching me to begin, begin now...whip him, hurt him now. "Please...please, Mistress Shadow."

I circle the whip to the side of me in mid-air. "Then turn over onto your stomach. And I'm warning you. No. Rustling. The. Sheet."

He changes position. Of course, the sheet crackles, more than it should have, and, on cue, Mr Delirious' body convulses, and dry sobs leave his mouth in a spew of sound.

"Oh, *really*, Simon. Is it *that* bad? Have you been *that* naughty since I last saw you?" I thwack the whip on the edge of the bed between his splayed legs, and he jumps.

Giggles switch places with his sobs. "Yes, Mistress Shadow. I have been a very naughty boy."

"Right. Up on all fours! Get that little arse up in the air. Now!"

He complies, the rustle of the sheet loud, and his hand massages his cock for one, two, three strokes before abandoning its task to lay flat against the bed. A high whimper rends the air, and I fancy the sound bounces off the steel table and ricochets around the dungeon.

"And now, fucker, you'll receive your punishment."

I arc the whip through the air. Force from my swing creates a buzzing noise, and the straps meet his arse in an eye-watering union. His breath hitches, he snaps his head back, and a pitiful wail joins the remnants of his previous whimper.

"Harder, Mistress Shadow. Faster."

His hands remain palm down on the bed, but I know soon, soon he'll snatch at his cock and pump until pre-cum dribbles down the tip. Whip meets flesh again and again, the time between lashes shorter. Strangled gasps, grunts, and ecstatic sighs stumble over one another at the top end of the bed, and Mr Delirious remains true to form and grips his penis.

"I-I... It's time for Mistress Darkness. Please." He takes his bony hand from his dick and slaps it against the bed, hangs his head, breathes deep. "I-I want...I want Mistress Darkness...to stand in front of me so I can...lick" — he pauses to pant — "her cunt."

Thwack!

"Is there anything else you want, filthy boy?"

His arse, red welts rising, gains a deep red hue. He scrunches his toes, squeezes his hands into fists, and I wonder how high his desire rates on the pleasure scale.

"I want you to...to stab those heels of yours into my arse cheeks." He grips his cock again. "Smack me with the soles. Hurt...me."

"Mistress Darkness!" I shout—*Thwack! Thwack!*—and, having known she would be needed, my co-worker and roomie saunters into the dungeon.

"Yes?" she asks.

"Bad boy here wants to lick you. Lick you until you come, loud and hard against his face."

Mr Delirious' tinny laughter indicates his mounting excitement, and I make eye contact with Darkness and jerk my head in the direction of the opposite end of the bed.

I raise the whip and bring it down as hard as I'm able. The contact of straps on skin buckles my knees.

Blonde Mistress Darkness, naked from the waist down, a tassel bra covering her large tits, sashays beside the bed, her derriere to Delirious' left. He stares at the smooth arse cheek and darts his tongue out, licks his lips. She bends and—*crack!*—turns a handle beneath the bed to lower the head end to enable our client to lave her clit until she comes, screaming.

She stands opposite me now, her pussy level with his mouth, but not close enough for him to touch.

"What do you say to me, Mr?" she asks.

I raise the whip, hold it steady, and gauge when he'll verbally respond.

He takes in a breath. "Th—" *Thwack, thwack, thwack!* "Ahhhhhhh!"

"What? What did you say?" I yell.

"Th-thank you, Mistress Darkness, Mistress Shadow. Thank you."

Darkness steps forward, the tops of her thighs against the edge of the bed, her slit ready for Delirious' tongue. "Lick me, fucker. Lick me until I come." Her eyes glaze, and she tilts her head back, lowers her lids, and grips the corners of the leather mattress. "Now!"

He buries his mouth in her mound. Our client receives four more lashes, and Darkness lets go of the bed to grab a breast in each hand, her nipples stiff, the areolas puckered. She massages, lifts her hips to give Delirious better access, and her mouth drops open.

"Ahhh...ahhhh. Mr, you're a bad, bad boy," she rasps.

This session never fails to arouse her. A primal force grips me—the urge to throw down the whip and get this episode over and done with. I quickly wrench off my boots, the gimp mask, and free my hair.

"Yes. I'm a bad"—his breathing escalates, and he fumbles for his cock, finds it, and masturbates...hard—"bad boy. Ahh. Uhh. Mistress Shadow...make me bleed."

My boot heel greets his right arse cheek, punctures the shiny welts, and a dribble of blood drips down the curve to disappear into the cleft.

The plastic sheet crackles. Semen spurts in a straight line to smack against the sheet—three, four, five shots—and Darkness screams through her orgasm. Mr Delirious lowers his face until his forehead rests against the bed, his hand still, his cock already deflating. Darkness' pussy glistens, juices matting the hairs around her clit, and she opens her eyes and stares at me.

I breathe hard and fast, legs apart, whip by my side. Mr Delirious begins to laugh his usual after-ejaculation laugh. He scuttles to the changing room and closes the curtain, his giggles high-pitched, manic, as though insanity has touched him.

Darkness walks towards me. "Do you have time for a chat after he's gone?"

"I do."

"Good."

The curtain being drawn back stops me wondering what she wants to chat about.

"Ooh! Ooh! Have I interrupted a *moment*?" Delirious asks.

I drop my hands by my sides, and Darkness disappears into my changing room.

"No," I say and fold the plastic sheet ready for disposal. "I'll see you next month perhaps." I want him out of here. Now. But there is one more thing he must do before he leaves.

He laughs again, the sound low at first, growing to a crescendo of crazy proportions. He rests his forehead on my hands, laughs so hard his shoulders shake. Then, as though the use of his windpipe is no longer possible, all sound cuts off, and he stands, sober of face and demeanour. "Goodbye."

He grabs up his whip and exits the room, leaving me reeling a little at how quickly his session went by. I pad into my dressing room, Darkness awaiting my presence on my leather beanbag, legs splayed, the finger of one hand circling a nipple, the pointer finger of her other inside her.

"Do you *have* to?" I say. "You've only just had an orgasm."

"Where were you last night?"

"Out." I don't want to tell her. Want to keep my meeting Luke to myself. I usually share everything with Darkness, but this time? No.

"Out? Not going to share where?"

"No." I lean against the doorjamb, ignoring the way she's fondling herself.

"Oh, okay."

There isn't time to talk further. Darkness will have to wait until later or tonight to talk about whatever's pissing her off...and something is.

"You have to go. I have another client coming. I need to get changed."

The air seems to vibrate, grow thick with tension. I feel stupidly annoyed with Darkness being here, her questions like accusations, different from her usual enquiries. Maybe I'm imagining that. Maybe because this thing with Luke is so new, so unbelievable, I want to hold it to myself a little longer.

No *maybe* about it.

Darkness stands and regards me for a few seconds...uncomfortable seconds that seem to stretch on forever.

"You're different," she says and walks out.

Chapter Six

Masochist

Some clients act as though it's my fault they have such desires. I suppose it makes it easier to cope with. To blame someone else means it isn't their fault. If truth be told, I don't think fault lies anywhere. We are what we are. After all, who am I to judge? I chose the career path of sating sexual needs. I have no doubt in my mind that I am perceived as strange. Sick, even.

```
Name: Matthew Scott
Preference: Butt-plug fucks, anal dildo
insertion, vocal degradation. Rubber nun's
outfit.
Notes: Also known as Mr Grouchy, Mr Scott appears
to detest his visits at first. Married. Two small
children.
```

I've often wondered why Mr Grouchy opted for the nun's outfit as his preference. He may have been brought up in a strict religious household. Maybe my nasty talk, coming from one who wears the disguise of someone so pure, gives him a degree of control over what he has been taught? Or possibly it's his way of flipping the bird at Christianity? I'll never know unless I ask, and to be honest, I'm not sure I want to know. To wonder is one thing, to know for sure is another.

The black mini-dress, a snug fit, barely conceals. My cleavage, arse, and stocking-clad legs lay bare, a feast for Matthew's eyes. In his rapture, he never fails to reach behind him in an attempt to touch me, to break one of the rules I've set. His stubbornness in this area inflames my tongue to unleash a barrage of vitriolic spew, a stream of words that heightens his desire.

My wimple is the last item I put on. It makes my head sweat, and the need to scratch my scalp entices further hurtful talk. Perhaps Mr Grouchy's reasoning behind my clothing isn't anything to do with his upbringing. A method to his madness?

The stairs outside my dungeon creak. The sound heralds either Matthew or Mistress Darkness' next client, the voluptuous Miss Robyn Sykes, whose fondness for nipple electrocution must strike the match of jealousy inside Darkness' male clients. They can't watch, can't join in, and Darkness telling them all about what she gets up to probably makes them come during the night when they grip their dicks while the wife is asleep. Miss Sykes pays double the price for her sessions—her way of further ensuring her anonymity here? The paparazzi would have the proverbial field day if they found out the girl-next-door model with the penetrative blue eyes comes here once a month to have her tits zapped and her clit licked.

Precise footsteps mince past my door and halt six paces on. More creaking equals no time to dwell. An impatient set of raps rattle my door, and I glance at the clock. Matthew, on time, waits for my command to enter and swings open the door.

Even with him around six-four, his formidable frame—as well as his sour demeanour—extorts no apprehension now. Upon first meeting Matthew, I entertained a brief scenario of having to run for the panic button that alerts Madam we're in trouble, but to my surprise, I've grown to like this grumpy, growling man.

He closes the door and places his payment on the small table. He grunts a greeting, appraises me from head to stiletto-covered toes, and stalks to the changing room. The sound of the curtain snapping across brings a smile to my lips, as does the shuffle of him discarding his clothing—Levi's, white cotton shirt, brown boots, and black leather jacket.

Matthew is a good-looking blond in his mid-thirties. If I'd spotted him in a bar before I met Luke, I'd have considered approaching him with a view to dates and a possible relationship. His wedding ring put me off, though.

Funny how it doesn't when he's in my dungeon.

A shriek from next door indicates Miss Sykes has received her first surge of electricity. I turn my thoughts to using the double-dick dildo. I've always said I wouldn't step over the line and share myself with my clients, but deriving pleasure from a sex toy and not Matthew doesn't count, does it?

He enters the dungeon, naked except for a gold chain and cross around his neck. His large hands would fit nicely over my breasts, and his round-tipped fingers could quite possibly encourage an orgasm if they tweaked my nipples rough and hard. And at one time I even thought about his lips, full and soft against my clit…but not now.

No. Only Beautiful Luke can have that pleasure.

"Kneel on the bed, face-down, sinner," I say.

Matthew furrows his brow and forms his mouth into a downward-pointing comma. He grouses but complies, gripping the sides, his knees near the edge of the bottom end. I place my foot on the pedal that lowers the bed and pump it so his arsehole is level with my vagina.

"How big do you want it, sinner?"

"I don't want it," he growls and hangs his head to rest on the bed.

I smile but sigh inwardly. "So what are you doing here, freak?"

"I-I'm...I'm here for you to punish me."

"Pardon? Have you forgotten your manners, Mr Scott?"

He pants—fighting against what he really wants?—and whispers, "Mistress Shadow."

"That's better. So, you don't want it, yet you're here for it. Rather contradictory as usual, aren't you, cocksucker?"

"I'm not a cocksucker," he says, his tone hard, insulted.

"Ah." I walk to the left wall and select a double-dick dildo. "That's right. You're a cock-*taker*, aren't you?"

He shifts position, and I wonder for a second if my jibes will one day lure him off the bed and into his clothes, never to return here again.

He stays put.

"No, I don't take cock."

I unhook the dildo from its hanger, grab a condom, and walk to the foot of the bed. While stepping into the dildo straps, I shout, "You don't take cock *what*?"

He grunts once more, his agitation obvious—he squeezes the bed sides, and his knuckles whiten. "I don't take cock, *Mistress Shadow*."

I shift my thong's gusset aside. The shorter rubber cock fits inside me, and I take a deep breath and imagine Beautiful Luke fills me. I'm wet, so wet. I sashay to the right side of the room to the steel table, the cock inside me slick against my juicy walls. The pressure from the heavier, larger dick that will slip inside Matthew's arse rubs against my clit, and I bite my lower lip.

I want you, Luke. Not him.

"Head up! Look at me!" I snap.

His narrowed gaze meets mine. Hatred swirls amid the brown irises, yet that down-turned comma mouth has flipped the other way. His smirk alerts me to the fact he still hasn't accepted his reason for being here—hasn't come to terms with the inevitable, isn't ready to play properly.

I sigh. "Put the condom on my cock, sinner."

He flares his nostrils. "I'm not touching that."

Another sigh from me. "Your denial bugs the fuck out of me, Mr Scott. You want it. You want my long, black cock rammed up your arse. Only you're not man enough to admit it, dirtbag."

His eyes form slits, and he clenches his jaw.

"You're nothing but a weedy, puny little arsehole who loves the thought of a nun shagging your back passage. I'll bet you imagine me as a man, don't you, Mr Scott? Married with two children, you probably give the impression you're a homophobe, when all along you fantasise about dicks probing your anus, dicks in your mouth, dicks, dicks, dicks..."

His cock grows hard and bobs. He rests on one hand and slaps my cock with the other. "Get that thing away from me."

"Away from you? *Away*? Why, don't you always want it *in* you? Pumping, rubbing against your G-spot? Doesn't its insertion make you grab your cock and masturbate until you spurt cum all over my bed?"

He shifts, leans on both elbows, and snatches the condom, rolling it over the pointed head and down my shaft. The movements jolt the smaller prick further inside me, and I savour the sensation, again wishing it was Luke.

Miss Sykes squeals. Darkness releases a short, sharp scream.

"There, that wasn't so difficult, was it?" I release another breath through pursed lips. I must get through this.

He lowers his head again, his arse in the perfect position, and I walk to stand behind him.

"Hmmm. Shall we go straight for the big one, or does my little cock-taker want a smaller one to start him off?"

Abruptly, he pushes himself upright and strokes his cock in a soft, slow rhythm and clenches his butt cheeks.

"Leave it alone until I *tell* you to touch it." I poke his lower back.

He flops forward, braces himself in his previous position. "I'm ready to take the big one straight off, Mistress Shadow."

His puckered hole winks.

"Ah, so *now* you admit you like to take it up the arse? Well, you'll have to wait while I apply the lube, won't you?"

He sighs and snarls, "Will you give it to me hard, Mistress Shadow?"

At the steel table, I ignore him, squeeze lube into my palm, and coat my large cock, eyes closed, imagining what it's like to be a man. Though I obviously gain no sensation from the cock itself, the one inside me moves in and out, and visions of Beautiful Luke standing before me, his hands outstretched to cup my tits almost sends me over the edge. I hold my breath, open my eyes, and move to stand behind Mr Scott once more.

The tip of one cock kisses his arse while the tip of the other greets the opening of my womb. Matthew gasps, paws the sides of the bed, and I'm almost certain he's clenching his teeth.

"Ready, sinner?"

He clears his throat. "Oh, yes, Mistress Shadow. I'm ready. Ride my arse. Please."

Slow and easy now, I push the tip against his opening, pressing with more force until it opens enough to clutch the head of my cock. The downy hairs in his arse crack shimmer, sweat-laden. To gain more leverage, I hold the bottom corners of the bed and insert the black rubber a millimetre at a time.

He squirms. His loud swallows mingle with the cries of ecstasy from next door. My heart pounds faster, and I shirk away the images of Darkness atop Miss Sykes, electric clamps removed, their breasts glossy with baby oil, gyrating against one another, squelching, nipples tight buds that rasp the other woman's tits.

Beautiful Luke takes their place in my mind, his prick hard and ready for me. I ease my cock deeper inside Matthew until I'm halfway in. The dick in my cunt—it's Luke, oh yes, it's Luke—moves further in with each of my minute pushes, and I long to ride Matthew's arse right now so that Luke can penetrate me hard and fast. But I must wait, enter Mr Scott languidly, until he's taken all of this rubber member and accustomed himself to it inside him.

"Does it feel good, sinner? Does my cock excite you?"

Push, push, push.

"Y-yes, Mistress Shadow."

"I'm going to fuck your arse so hard—"

"Uh, Uh, Mistress Shadow—"

Thrust, thrust, thrust.

"Don't you *dare* come too soon, fucker. Wait, dammit!"

I give him a stinging slap to his right arse cheek, and he barely moves in case my cock pops out of its new home.

"Fucking wait, dimwit! Do you understand?"

I allow his groan as a response and shove deeper. The pressure inside me triples, and with one quick jerk, I fill him. Mistress Darkness' animalistic screeches fill my ears—I'd recognise them anywhere—and Matthew slides his hands to lay flat on the bed. He kneads the leather, and his breathing grows rapid.

"Ready, Mr Scott?"

"Oh, yes. Yes, Mistress Shadow."

I pull out, push in—out, in, out—a frantic rhythm that evinces a wolfish howl from Matthew and a gasp of pleasure from me. Luke is inside me—he pumps, fucks my hole, the base of the cock in Matthew's arse stimulating my clit. Mistress Darkness nears her peak—the noises from her dungeon blend with the sounds in mine. I let go of the bed and slap my palms against my rubber-covered breasts, caress them with hard fingers, pretend Luke's hands bring the pleasure.

Matthew lifts his right hand from the bed and sneaks it backwards, fingers questing to touch me, any part of me.

"Don't you even think of touching me, you piece of shit. How"—thrust—"fucking"—push—"dare you!"

He jerks his hand away and in the direction of his cock.

"And do *not* touch yourself, dirty sinner boy. You touch and I pull out, do you understand?"

I fuck him harder, indulge in a satisfied smile as he bobs his head up and down in agreement, and allow the final, pinnacle-achieved yell from Mistress Darkness to encompass me in its carnality.

My head itches.

"Pump your cock and make yourself come, shit-for-brains. Go on, grip it, fuck it with your hand. Come for me, come..."

Matthew's hand finds its home, and I lean to the right to watch him yank the foreskin back and forth, back and forth. He snaps his head up, his butt cheeks splayed, and I massage my tits, the sensation of the rubber inside my hole urging me to climax. Wetness coats the tops of my inner thighs, and the musky scent of sex reaches my nose.

"Can you smell me, Mr Scott? Can you smell how much this pure, innocent little nun wants you to splash your semen onto her bed? Harder, Matthew. Harder. Faster."

In sync with my movements, Matthew's hand works quicker. The veins on his wrists bulge, and the pulse in my clit strengthens as I chase the goal.

And it arrives, that crash, that sensation of riding a rollercoaster over and down a metal hill, and I manage to hold all sound inside—not a whimper, not a loud exhalation of breath.

Matthew comes, his yell muffled under the pounding in my ears, and his cum smacks against the leather like my earlier slap to his arse. His heavy exhalations infiltrate the fog in my mind and snap me back to attention. I withdraw my cock, the inside of the panty area wet with my juices, and discard the condom in a nearby bin.

My client—back arched, held up by one hand, his other dangling over the side of the bed—heaves in a giant breath and raises himself up. "Thank you, Mistress Shadow."

"You're welcome, Mr Scott." I toss him some tissues, some wet wipes, and instruct him to clean up and dress. After picking up my payment, I enter my changing room, close the door, and lean my back against it.

Make this day go faster. Please.

Chapter Seven

Satyriasis

Many men will claim they'd love to indulge in sex more than once a day, but for one of my clients, satyriasis has taken over his life. He thinks of nothing but sex for the majority of his day and must act on the impulse to have intercourse. He brings Madam a lot of business, visiting one of us at least once a day. One man's affliction is our monetary gain. Heartless, aren't I?

```
Name: Roger Liston
Preference: Anything goes.
Notes: I have found Mr Liston to be an amenable
character, though I always feel I have let him
down by refusing to indulge in intercourse with
him. He seems to like my sessions, but I would
bet my last penny he would rather be with
Mistress Darkness. After all, they're two of a
kind.
```

I peel off my black, PVC, all-in-one suit and the dildo, then take a shower. Mr Scott doesn't like the feel of skin-on-skin as I pump into his arse.

"The squeak of the fabric enhances my desire," he'd said. "Makes me come harder."

I don't question, just do my best to accommodate his whims. Though now things have changed between me and Luke, I'm beginning to wonder if this career is the right one for me. I know Luke said he doesn't mind, but...

Sighing, I push him from my mind. I should really see whether we even get into a relationship before considering ditching my job. I'm jumping the damn gun but I can't help it.

I want to be Ursula all the time.

It's time to concentrate on the session to come.

Mr Liston asks that I greet him naked, though I've never been able to bring myself to grant his request. Instead, I select the usual attire for him — a red rubber thong, matching nipple tassels, and red high-heeled shoes. My cunt is covered to some degree, as is my face, though only partially. The red eye mask is enough to conceal my identity. Mr Liston prefers anonymity. Heaven forbid he should see one of us on the street. Recognition, if only between ourselves, would ensure his secret is no longer safe, at least in his mind.

He told me once that his wife sates his desires twice a day, has done for the past five years, but she can't tolerate any more than that. Mr Liston needs his wants met at least seven times in twenty-four hours.

His latest instructions over the telephone were the same as they always are. I must stand at the bottom of the bed and await his arrival. Once he's knocked, I have to run — yes, run so he hears my heels clacking on the tiled floor — into my dressing room and stare at him through the two-way mirror in my door.

While I wait, I run my fingers through my hair and savour the feeling as it swishes against my bare back. I smooth my hands down my torso — to rid myself of the previous client? I don't know — it's a habit I've developed over the past few months — and walk over to the sink at the far end of the steel table to wash my hands.

Mr Liston's tread, loud and heavy, stomps on the stairs, and the steps creak louder than they do with any other client. He said once that he stamps on purpose so I know exactly when to run.

He knocks, and the door rattles in its frame.

I must *not* say enter. I must *not* act dominant until he says so. With my other clients, the role is reversed, it's my job to act that way. So why do I allow Mr Liston to control me? Perhaps because I have an understanding of his condition? Darkness has tried to explain nymphomania to me, how she can have meaningful intercourse with someone she cares about, yet switch off her emotions and shag anything that moves so long as it quenches her thirst for sex. Those desires rage through her to the point where she can quite literally grab anyone off the street and fuck them.

Hence this job being a perfect fit for her.

I run to my dressing room and slam the door.

Almost immediately, Mr Liston enters the room and yells, "Honey, I'm home!" — part of the illusion that he's fucking his wife and not being unfaithful. I watch him through the window. He wrenches off his grey suit jacket and throws it on a stool in the left corner by the door. Before he takes off his trousers, he pulls out his wallet and extracts some cash, placing it on the table.

Trousers around his ankles, he steps out of his pants with a little difficulty due to his shoes, and sends them sailing to rest with his jacket. His boxer shorts exhibit his proud erection, which juts out of the fly the moment he grips the waistband to yank the garment off. He kicks them to his other clothes, and, incongruous as he looks, he stoops to untie his shoelaces and slings his black shoes under the bed. His socks follow, as does his shirt and tie. He struts to the wall housing my instruments of torture and selects a long-stranded whip.

The next part never fails to fascinate me, and Mr Liston never fails to act it out. His ritual, his purging.

He stands at the bottom of the bed, his back to me, and flicks the whip over his shoulder. The strand's end cracks against his strong back, the contact leaving a red-raw welt. Again and again he whips himself and chants, "Dirty, naughty man. Dirty, naughty man."

I often feel sorry for him at this point. He must have to do this to enable him to continue with the session. He adores his wife and can't quite separate what he does with us with what he does with her. To him, sex is sex, whomever he does it with. Surely, though — like Darkness said — sex with his wife must have a deeper meaning?

After twenty lashes and some welts seeping blood, he places the whip on the floor and climbs on top of the bed.

"Come and see me, beautiful!"

My cue. I swing open the door in an exaggerated gesture and smile the smile of the ecstatic. I'm so happy my darling husband is home! I tiptoe over to the bed and stand by his side. Already he masturbates, his strokes hard and fast, the head of his cock red and engorged to the point of being sore.

"Darling! How lovely to see you." Gushing isn't my scene, but he tips big.

"Come and sit on my face." His smile widens, and his cheeks gain a red blush as his excitement mounts. Hand movements more frantic, he waits for my response — one he knows he'll receive, yet still he wishes, hopes for something more.

"Now, dear, you know I don't do things like that." I place my hands on my hips and stare down at him as though he's been the naughtiest man ever. "How about I tease you a little, hmm? Would you like me to do that?"

He nods and jerks his cock harder.

I move to the bottom of the bed and pump the pedal to lower it. Almost at floor level now, Mr Liston raises his head to get a better look at me. He narrows his eyes in lust, and his white-toothed grin gleams under the light.

"Stand over me. Take off your panties. Let me look at your hole." He winks.

I straddle the bed. "Darling, that isn't a polite thing for a lady to do, is it?"

He frowns for an instant but brightens his face with a smile. "No. No, I suppose it isn't, dear. Did you have a good day today?"

"I did. I cooked a stew and cleaned the house. I baked cookies. I did all the laundry." Inwardly, I sigh at his need for assurance that he's with his wife.

"You're wonderful. Now suck my cock."

"Why, Roger, what on earth is wrong with you?"

"Nothing. I just want to inject some fun into the bedroom." He fists his cock faster. "How do you feel about this suggestion? Pretend you're a dominatrix."

I act as if considering his request, rest one finger against my chin, and look at the ceiling. "I-I don't know if I could. I mean, I'm such a prude, Roger."

"Darling, trust me. You'll love it."

I giggle. "Oh, all right."

I shuffle backwards, tiptoe to the steel table, and hunker down, giving him a great view of my splayed arse cheeks. I open the top drawer of the filing cabinet and bring out what I always do. Mr Liston won't last long once I place the fake cunt near his cock.

I return to the bed, the faux vagina held behind me, and pump the pedal until the mattress is level with my pelvis. "So, you want a dominant wife, do you, Roger?"

"Yes!" He grips himself tighter, masturbates with more fervour. "Yes. What have you in mind, beautiful?"

"What about a threesome, hmm? I know how much you long for one of those. Shall I at last comply?"

"Yes, yes! Bring her in," he says, his voice almost pathetic, needy. He reaches for me, his fingertips brushing my right side.

"Oh! Hands off, remember." I step back, wag my finger at him, and my nipple tassels dance. "But you may touch our guest as much as you like."

I bring Miss Suzy out from behind my back and present her to him. He releases his cock and grabs her—a plastic arse, waist, and vagina with pubic hairs—and draws her to his face. He licks her clit. Precum glistens on his penis tip.

"Touch me. Touch me, Mistress Shadow." He laps faster, his tongue rasping against the hairs.

"No, I will not. Who do you think you are? How dare you talk to me that way?"

He closes his eyes, and I smile witnessing his rapture, his belief that there are two women with him now.

"Please. I beg you."

"No. You must plunge into Miss Suzy and fuck her ragged. Do it. Do as I say. Now!"

He pulls away from her clit and sits up, places her beneath him on the bed, and prepares to enter her hole.

"Use a condom, you filthy man!" I reach over to the steel table and pick up a condom, open its wrapper, and toss the rubber at him.

He sheaths himself quickly with one hand and slips into her, an easy insertion. He shudders with wild thrusts, one hand on the rubber handgrip attached to the centre of her waist.

"That's it. Ride the bitch." I step away from the bed and take stock of the time. As usual, Mr Liston is ahead of schedule.

"I'm riding her. Uh, yeah, I'm riding her good."

His arse cheeks clench with each push, and the time to call Mistress Darkness draws near.

"What about *another* woman?" I ask. "What about having my beautiful friend to join us?"

He nods, pumps harder into Miss Suzy, and gasps. "Be quick. I can't last much longer."

"Oh, Darkness!"

Darkness enters my dungeon, takes in the scene and smiles. She oozes sex appeal, naked as she is, and sways over to me, her enticing hips and full breasts begging for someone's — anyone's — touch. "Yes?" she asks, the epitome of innocence.

"My husband wished for a threesome. He got it." I nod at Miss Suzy. "He wished for my dominance. He got it. I suggested that you join us. What do you say?"

Her smile widens further, and she moves closer, so close one bare breast rubs against mine.

"Oh!" Mr Liston gasps, his gaze flicking from us to Miss Suzy. "Hurry!"

We step further along, level with his head, and adopt our positions, me standing, legs splayed, Darkness standing right in front of him, fretting her clit. Mr Liston widens his eyes and grasps Miss Suzy's handgrip tighter. His rhythm gains a faster pace, as does Darkness' fingers on her bud, and I close my eyes to what they're both doing.

Mr Liston's groan fills the room, and the sound of him inside Miss Suzy tells me he won't be long.

"Shadow," Darkness whispers, "lay on the floor."

I open my eyes and look at her. "For...?"

She smiles. "I want to lick you while you lick me. Now."

I shake my head. She tries this often, to see if I'll do what she asks when we're in the presence of a client. "No."

It's too late for giving Mr Liston a real show anyway. He grunts, moans, spurts into Miss Suzy and realises his fantasy once again.

"Uh-uh-uh," Liston grunts, then releases a primal yell.

He's spent, flopped over Miss Suzy, his back arched, fingers still clasped around her handgrip, forehead against the bed. Darkness comes loudly, fingers a feverish flicker of movement on her clit. Her body sags. I smile at her, wanting to take away the sting of my earlier refusal, and she returns it with one of her own, surprisingly shy.

"Ladies, that was truly wonderful," Mr Liston says, now on his side spooning Miss Suzy.

He's the last customer of my day, so it doesn't matter if we lounge here for five minutes, basking in the afterglow. Mr Liston still has half an hour of his session remaining. But I want them out of here. Now.

Thoughts wend through my mind, and I close my eyes, relishing the idea of meeting Luke later.

One day... One day soon he'll give himself to me, and in that instant, I imagine I'll walk away from this job forever and follow him to the ends of the earth.

Chapter Eight

Home

Darkness has gone out in search of someone to fuck, leaving me in our apartment alone. Waiting for the telephone to ring. To hear Luke's voice on the other end of the line, him telling me he's finished his work and we can meet. I'm on pins and needles. It's insane, the way I feel, all coiled up and ready to burst.

I've left my hair loose, have my little black skirt on, a short black blouse to match, and for a splash of colour, my high-heeled red stilettos. No bra, no panties. I don't want underwear in the way if —

The phone ringing, even though I've been expecting it, startles me. My stomach rolls, bunches, rolls again, and I swallow in an effort to stop myself throwing up. Not the nicest thing to happen just before meeting the man of my dreams, but there you have it. I'm nervous as hell. I've dreamed of this moment for so long now that the thought of it actually coming true has scared me senseless.

Jumping up from the sofa and dashing about flapping my arms isn't going to get that phone answered, so I take a deep breath and lift my mobile.

"Hello?" It has to be him. I can't imagine Darkness calling me for any reason, not at this time of night anyway.

"Hey, you."

I almost sink to the floor at the sound of those words. Luke has called, like he said he would. Had I doubted him? Yes, I had. Couldn't believe he'd stick to what he'd said, that he wanted to see me outside of the dungeon, but here he was, his breathing fast and juddery.

"Hey yourself," I say, going for nonchalance.

"I've finished. Do you still want—"

"Yes. Tell me your address." I surprise myself at my dominance while being just myself. The nerves, I'd thought they'd got the better of me, but apparently they haven't. I have to see him, be with him, and that alone spurs me into saying, "I can't wait to see you." If he knows just a little of how I feel about him, it might put him at ease.

He rattles off his address and I scribble it down on a note pad.

I am going to Luke's house, somewhere I never thought I'd go.

* * * *

He lives in quite a swanky dockside flat on the other side of London. On the journey, I'd wondered about how it would go, my mind conjuring scenarios of me pressing the doorbell and him letting me into the lobby. Or me stepping into an elevator, or taking the stairs, arriving at his actual front door breathless and full of anticipation.

It doesn't turn out that way.

I park up and get out of my car, inserting the key in the door to lock it. I suppose I should get a new car, one with a key fob that locks the door for me, but I just can't. If it isn't broke, don't fix it...

Luke stands in front of his building, a red-brick effort that screams class and money. The main double doors behind him, glass inside a steel frame, show passers-by a posh foyer with what looks like a maple reception desk. I can just about see a guy sitting behind it, black uniform jacket loose, as though he's undone the buttons, a peaked hat on his brown-haired head.

Luke has gone for casual. Blue jeans, white T-shirt. Bare feet.

The nerves rattle inside me again...until I meet Luke's gaze. Then they disappear, and I walk towards him as if I do this all the time. He smiles, a gentle quirk of his lips that does all manner of things to my insides. I smile back, so damn relieved tension hasn't made an appearance between us. I'd worried about that.

"Hi," he says as I reach him, drawing me close into a tight embrace. He rests his chin on top of my head, smoothes his hands up and down my back, and murmurs, "Part of me thought you might not come."

God, if he only knew... "How could I not come?" I push on, throwing my insecurities away. He *has* to know how I feel. "I've wished for this since the first time I saw you."

His heart rate kicks up beneath my cheek, and his scent, his glorious scent fills my nose.

"Shit. We've wasted so much time." He slides the fingers of one hand into my hair and strokes my scalp.

"But I'm here now. We can make up for it."

Did I just say that? Really?

"Come on. I'll take you up."

He releases me, holds my hand and leads me through the doorway and into the foyer. The uniformed guy looks up briefly, nods, then lowers his head, back to reading a book or whatever he's doing behind the highest part of the desk. I don't care. All I'm interested in is soaking up this experience, of having my hand clasped protectively in Luke's, being taken to his apartment.

The elevator ride, though spent in silence, isn't uncomfortable. Far from it. It's as though we're meant to be here, at ease in one another's company. Shadow is gone, and in her place stands Ursula, with more confidence than she's had before.

He wants me…

We step out of the elevator, Luke again leading the way. He takes me to a door at the far end of a long corridor, much like those in a hotel. A frisson of nerves remain in my belly, but other than that I'm relaxed, wanting to drown in this night and everything it has to offer. Will we eat? Drink wine? Fuck?

He inserts his key and swings the door open, allowing me to enter first. His place isn't anything like I expected. I thought it would be a mess, clothes strewn about, beer cans on the coffee table, among porn magazines and the TV remote control. His lifestyle, from what he'd told me he gets up to, made me think he was the kind of man to kick back and not care about anything but what he wanted.

How wrong I've been.

His living room is perfect, everything in its place. White walls and carpet, white everything, except for a few splatters of colour from jazzy throw pillows and bright turquoise curtains. A coffee table sits between two sofas opposite one another, and a white vase filled with a dozen or more red roses stands out starkly.

The door closes behind me, and I close my eyes in order to calm myself. It seems every time I think I've got myself under control I'm proved wrong. Each time something new happens, the nerves spark to let me know they're still there.

Luke comes to stand by my side, and for God's sake, my stomach bunches again.

"The flowers. They're for you. I'm not sure if you're a flowery kind of woman, but…"

"Thank you. They're beautiful." *Like you.*

"Would you like a drink? Something to eat? Please, sit down."

He's a gentleman, something I also hadn't expected. His usual manner in the dungeon has vanished, leaving behind a stranger — one I met in the gym, the pub, and then my car. Where has the burly Luke gone? I love him either way, and maybe his rough side will appear again after we've got to know one another better. I fell in love with him that way, and it would be a shame if he hid it, thinking I wanted a different kind of man.

I walk across the soft carpet, loving its gentle caress on my soles, and sit at one end of a sofa. It's so comfortable, I know I won't have any trouble relaxing here. I put my car keys on the table, wincing as they make a scraping sound, and check to see if they've scratched the surface. They haven't, and I release a quiet sigh of relief. I slip off my shoes and curl up in the corner, again, like I've done this before. I can't explain it, but part of me feels like I'm meant to be here. That I'm home.

Luke remains where I left him, staring at me, a small smile playing about his lips. "I never thought I'd see you here. It's...fuck, it's crazy. Didn't think you'd be interested in someone like me. Still can't believe it."

"I am here, and believe me, I can't believe this either."

Time passes, where we gaze at each other, no words necessary.

He breaks the spell by coming towards me, sitting close, facing me with one leg bent beneath him. Reaching out, he touches my thigh, watches as he moves his hand up the length and back down again to my knee as though he can't comprehend this is happening. I stare at what he's doing, feeling much the same. He's touching me like he really wants to, as if he's putting his dreams into action. I can't stop staring—unable, for a moment, to accept this is real. My heart thuds so hard it hurts, and a ball of emotion settles in my chest and throat. I want to cry, the happy kind where I'd laugh and splutter and feel giddy all at once. Where I'd thank my lucky stars and whatever else out there made this possible.

I think about that for a few seconds, mesmerised by his hand. I made this happen. Me—Ursula—not fate or destiny. But then, did fate send him my way in the first place? I don't know and can't think about it anymore because his hand...God, it sends shivers through me, and I want to lean forward and kiss him. I don't. He must make the move—the move that will tell me once and for all I'm not dreaming. I want him to be the one who takes it further.

Instead of pressing his lips to mine, he says, "I've been with so many women, searching... And here you are, been there for me all along." He shakes his head. "I'm not normally so...nervous. Just take what I want.

But you? Shit, you've gone and turned me upside down."

Throwing my previous thoughts out the window, I cup his cheek, draw his face to mine and, with eyes still open, kiss him tenderly. If he needs assurance, then that's what he'll get. If he needs some sign that I want him...

He parts his lips at the same time as he closes his eyes, and groans as I slide my tongue inside, exploring the contours of his mouth. I close my eyes, too, revelling in the sensations spiralling through me. A rush of pleasure sweeps from my toes right to my cunt, and I suddenly want his fingers, his cock there...now.

Taking the initiative, I push him back against the sofa and straddle him, kissing with more urgency. My nipples harden, and God, I want to feel him slip inside me. I'm wet for him, soaked with need, and I want him to smell how much he's turning me on.

He settles his hands on my waist, groaning again—a rough, strained sound that brings a fresh stream of juice to my folds. I press myself to his erection, whimpering at the feel of its hardness. I haven't had sex in the longest time, waiting for this moment, but damn, I'm ready for him to fill me up and fuck me senseless.

Unable to wait for him to make the next move, I lift the hem of his T-shirt, breaking my mouth from his to drag the fabric over his head. Lips back on his, tongue searching, I smooth my hands down his bare torso. The smattering of hairs rasp on my palms, and an acute spike of ecstasy burns my cunt. My clit throbs. I need him to lick it, touch it, rub it with his cock, do anything to bring me release.

Kissing his jawline, his cheek, I whisper against his skin between pecks, "Fuck me, Luke. Fuck me hard and fast."

"Oh, fuck. Jesus. Let me look at you."

I sit up and gaze down at him, see the smouldering lust in his eyes and work open his jeans button, pull down the zip. His cock springs free, no underwear holding it captive, and I smile at the thought that we both declined to wear any. I grip his dick. The feel of him, the hardness of his length and his soft skin, is almost more than I can bear. My clit reacts with violent thudding, and my nipples grow so taut they're almost painful.

He wastes no time then. My blouse is removed and thrown God knows where, the loss of his cock in my hand a wrench. He slides his hands around to pop open the button of my skirt. It loosens enough for him to shove the skirt from my thighs up to my waist, and he stares down at everything I have to offer. Sucks in a breath.

"Christ, you smell good."

He brings his hands back around front and rubs my thighs, fingertips skimming the outer flesh of my labia then drawing his hands lower again, a maddening tease. I watch him, then take his dick in hand once more. With slow movements, I drag my hand up and down, loving the way he expands, the way his tip bulges. His vein pulses, his need for me clear and hard, and fuck, I can't hold off any longer. I rise up and lean forward, positioning his tip at my entrance, pressing my breasts against him. The skin-on-skin contact drives me insane.

"Wait," he says and fumbles between the sofa cushions, bringing out a condom. "I'd hoped..." he says by way of explanation, covering his cock with the rubber.

I don't answer but ease down, letting him fill me slowly. His girth stretches my inner walls, his length just about fitting inside me. My cunt rim burns a little with the intrusion, but I love it, love every damn bit of it. I moan once he's fully inside, and sit still, taking in the feel of him before gently moving at a steady pace. I sit back to look at him, and he stares at where we join, eyes wide, flicking his tongue out to lick his lower lip.

"Fuck, that looks so damn hot. Feels so good. Christ, Ursula…"

He cups my breasts, thumbs playing over my sensitive nipples, and I up the pace. It's too much — him inside me, his hands on me — and I have an urgent need to race to the finish line, to have an orgasm crash over me and sweep me away. His touch grows stronger, as though his desire has given him the courage to fondle faster, harder.

"More," I whisper. "Pinch me, rub me. Harder. Just…more."

He complies, massaging, tweaking, lifting his hips to seat himself further inside. "Ah, that's…this is… I can't hold off much longer."

Hands on his shoulders, I jam down onto him, wanting a furious fuck. It may be fast, but damn, I'm not about to let him forget me in a hurry. Up and down, up and down. His hands and fingers working my breasts and nipples. Him leaning forward to slide his tongue down the column of my neck, breath hot on my skin. Me taking one hand from his shoulder and seeking out my clit. It's burning, needs my speedy fingers to rub, to help me reach that place I can't wait to be.

"Ah, Jesus. You touching yourself. So fucking sexy," he rasps. "Faster. I'm nearly there. Faster."

I obey, almost there myself. He pinches my nipples, twists and pulls, and I'm undone. Pleasure zips from my hard buds right into the centre of me, and with my busy fingers between my legs, I let the pressure build. Wait for it to burst.

It does, in an enormous wave of pleasure that takes my breath away for several seconds. I gasp for air, suck it inside, then release it — groan-laden, raw with desire. Luke moans, jerks his hips, shunting his cock in as far as it can go. Bliss spirals inside, erupting on the outside, radiating from my clit to my entire slit.

"Oh, God. That's it, Luke. I'm there…"

In response, he moans again and tweaks my nipples harder, dipping his head to suck one into his mouth. The wetness of his mouth, his tongue swirling, makes my orgasm thunder through me, weakening my arms and legs and sending me light-headed.

"Shit. Fuck," I shout. "Yes, fucking yes!"

He pulls back on my nipple, biting lightly before letting it go. "Tight, so fucking tight…" He grips my waist, directing my speed, thrusting up as he smacks me back down again.

I let him take over, digging my nails into his shoulder. His cum spurts into the condom, hot and heavy. I open my eyes to watch him. The cords on his neck stand out as he grits his teeth, a series of strangled groans seeping through them.

"Ah, ah, Jesus, woman!"

I moan, breathing stuttered, head dizzy, the last waves of pleasure ebbing and flowing beneath my fingertips. "This… God, I love you. Want you."

He lifts his head, and I tilt mine to kiss him as his cock pulses and hardens a little more with another

Natalie Dae

ejection of cum. I love the way he's slamming me onto him, lifting me up with those big hands of his. My breasts bounce then squash against him, the friction delicious on my nipples. Sweat drips down the centre of my back. My pussy throbs with aftershocks. Another hard jerk of Luke's hips, another wrench downward on his cock, and he stops moving me. A gravelly groan leaves him, and he takes his mouth away to bite down on my shoulder.

Out of breath, reeling from the sensations still weaving through my cunt, I rest my forehead on his shoulder and look down at where our bodies are joined. He kisses where he'd bitten me, laves his tongue over the spot. My pulse thuds so hard in my ears, and my chest strains from my heaving breaths.

That was one fast and crazy fuck. The best of my life so far.

I push up, weave my fingers into his hair, and look into his eyes.

"Fuck, you're beautiful," he says, lightly caressing one breast. "So damn beautiful."

I smile, thinking of what I've always called him. I wish then, with every bit of me, that we'll go somewhere, that a wonderful relationship is right around the corner. "As are you, Beautiful Luke."

"You'll stay?" He looks at me hopefully.

"I'll stay." My heart almost bursts with love for him.

"And we'll make a go of it?"

I think of my job versus where I am now, still seated on his glorious cock, his hands on my breasts. There's nowhere else I'd rather be. My job can go and take a running jump if it makes things awkward between us. I'll do something different, make a completely new start. Cane his feet when he feels the need. Do whatever he asks of me in the bedroom. After all, I have the experience and know-how. And if he doesn't mind what I do, if it turns him on, then I'll continue.

A whole new world awaits us.

I nod. "We'll make a go of it. Forever."

Part Two

Mistress Darkness

Chapter Nine

Hunger
12th June – Morning

    This hunger, it eats at me, plagues my life with its dominance. If it pertained to food, I'd manage the affliction by eating and exercising the calories away. But hell, my hunger is for sex. As much of it as I can get. There. I've fully admitted it to myself. They say the first step to getting better is admittance, though I don't know how doing so will enable me to get better. Can I get better? Is medication available for this? So far, I've given in to my desires and fed the beast that sends pulses to my clit, feeds my mind with images of carnal delights so that I have to act on them, play them out.

    I bless the day I met Mistress Shadow. She sauntered up to Madam's reception desk as though she'd been there before and glanced at me signing in for work. Pure lust dominated me at that moment, and ever since then I've hoped she'd help me out during the times I can't find a man to fuck me.

    But I can hardly expect her to sate all of my desires...or any of them. She understands my predicament, why I have sex with all of my clients, but she's hooked on the man she calls Beautiful Luke. There's no room for me in her life like that. She looks at me as though she loves me as much as I love her. But she doesn't. No. She loves me as much as she is able, as a friend, but I'm under no illusion — she'd prefer Beautiful Luke over me any day.

Well, that's enough from me this morning. The work day begins in half an hour. I have Mr Lewis for my first client. Too exciting.

I want to feel what Shadow feels, even though a fuck with Mr Lewis is hardly the same thing. Shadow and Luke have love.

I don't.

```
Name: Mr Harvey Lewis
Preference: Nipple tweaks, arse slapping, hair
pulling.
Notes: Enjoys a wide variety of positions, though
he prefers me on top.
```

Harvey has been my client for the past six months. We've built up a good rapport over that time, and, of course, even though it isn't exactly allowed, Madam sent him to me straight off as he'd enquired as to whether her girls offered any 'extras'.

Madam is a kind but strict woman. She holds us in the utmost regard, cares for us better than if we were her daughters. She runs a tight ship, and all clients, whether they have sex here or not, must undergo tests to ensure we're always safe from any diseases. However, those of us who do cross the line must always wear a condom, and if we're found going bareback, we're out of a job.

Mr Lewis, married for fifteen years to a socialite who flits from modelling venues to high-profile nightspots, visits me for what she can't give him. Unabridged sex—no stipulations, no clauses, and no strings. The only thing against him is the time limit, though he has booked a two-hour session before after his wife forced abstinence on him for a week.

Harvey, hot-blooded and a pleasure to service, shouldn't have his needs denied...otherwise, he wouldn't fuck me. He says he doesn't see anyone else. I'm his mistress of sorts, though I don't see him outside of these walls. I would, given that he's appealing to the eye—blond and well-muscled. Nevertheless, his wife's prominence doesn't allow it. His association with her leaves him open to the paparazzi chasing him for as many photo opportunities as they do her. It seems no one believes a good-looking man would stay faithful, however beautiful and voluptuous his wife may be. And in his case they'd be right.

His knock on the door quickens my heartbeat, and I fluff my long blonde hair, smooth my outfit—a transparent pink baby-doll negligee that leaves nothing to the imagination. My nipples, clearly visible, peak against the sexy fabric, and I close my eyes and inhale one last, calming breath before he enters.

And there he stands, framed in the doorway, his ridiculous disguise laugh-worthy. A black Afro wig sits on his head, his all-in-one, bell-bottom trouser suit reminiscent of the seventies. He told me he parks his car in a woodland clearing on the way here and changes from his usual clothing, cramped in his two-seater sports car. I've often wondered what he would do should he be followed by the press and get caught wearing such a silly get-up. What excuse could he give?

"Sorry, can't chat, I'm on my way to a fancy dress party."
"At nine in the morning, sir?"

I smile at the image and hold out my hand. He steps forward and takes it, his skin soft and warm. He caresses my wrist with the pad of his thumb.

"Hello, Harvey."

"Morning, Princess."

He pulls me towards him and engulfs me in his hard, solid embrace. Roams his hands over my back, massages my shoulders, and strokes my neck.

"What do you fancy today?" I whisper against his lips.

He doesn't answer but tugs me into my changing room and, with a flick of his head, indicates he wants me splayed on the red leather beanbag bed, as usual. The red walls and low lighting give him a demonic appearance—all good. It adds to the spice of the moment, the naughtiness. I lay down, legs open, toes pointed outwards, arms relaxed at my sides. I wiggle my arse deeper into the bag and prepare to watch him undress.

He should have been a stripper.

Mr Lewis faces away from me and bends over, affording me a fantastic view of his toned arse, albeit covered in silky fabric. His absurd black platform boots come off, and he tosses them to the side, their clonk loud as they meet the floor. The sound of his zip opening from neck to crotch rips through the still air, and a glimpse of his tawny chest hair whets my appetite further, but *wets* something else a whole lot more. He removes the wig. My clit throbs—has done since I awoke this morning—and I'm glad I didn't masturbate before work. It would have taken the edge off this session. Harvey peels his suit from his body and kicks it skyward, where it falls in a heap beside me. No other clothing remains on his body.

What a cock. Long and wide with a purple-hued head—erect, it leans away from his pelvis, the weight of it begging to be inside me, thrusting in and out of my cunt until I scream.

"Fuck, I want you," I mutter and move my hand to my labia, fingers searching the soft, delicate folds, finding my clit, hard and aching.

His smile ignites a thrill in the pit of my stomach for what is to come, and just to tease him, I move my other hand beneath my negligee and fondle my breasts.

If I'm not careful, I'll come.

He strides towards me and straddles my waist, his breaths hot and sweet against the side of my neck. Shit, he's too damn sexy.

"I wanted you all last night," he whispers in my ear. "At that boring party, I thought of nothing but you. Your tits, your arse, your tight hole. I couldn't sleep. Couldn't wait until this morning."

He peppers my neck and collarbone with feather-light kisses and dashes his tongue out to leave a damp trail down to the neckline of my lingerie. I long to close my eyes, but watching him turns me on more. With his teeth, he nips the end of one of the ribbons that ties my outfit at the front. The bow now undone, Harvey nestles his mouth between the open fabric and laves a path with his tongue across one breast, latching onto a taut, sensitive nipple. Holding it between his teeth, he flashes his tongue across the tip.

Ripples of pleasure surge down to join those in my clit, and I stop masturbating in case I come. I place my hand at the base of his spine and stroke him, the transfer of my juices to his skin producing an electrified jolt. I want him to smell of me, for my scent to bloom with the heat of the shower afterwards and make him smile, make him recall our passion as he washes all traces of me away until next week.

Harvey, his attention still on my breast, shifts position so his legs settle between mine. His hard cock presses against my centre, and he gyrates, rubs it up and down my opening. A low growl rumbles in his chest, and he frees my nipple. The cool air devours the wetness and hardens my nipple further, and an emptiness inside me at the removal of his mouth almost makes me want to cry in frustration. He clasps my waist with his strong hands, slaps my thigh.

Harvey winks, and a devilish smile curves his lips. His wide eyes, set in a tanned, handsome face, look down at me, the need for a good fuck swirling in their blueness. I reach to the side, beneath the beanbag, and search for the condom I'd placed there earlier. Ripping the packet with my teeth, I remove the sheath and roll it down his length. In seconds, I position his cock at my entrance.

"I'm going to ride you, Princess." Harvey palms my tits, kneads with his fingers, rough yet gentle.

He plunges in and fills me, fills me so fully I bite back a scream. His rigid hotness sears, and my cunt spasms, clenching around his width. My clit aches, and that thrill in my stomach intensifies, rips an acidic pleasure-path to my centre.

"Ah, fuck," I breathe and clasp his upper arms as he begins a slow rhythm—in, out, in, out—his touches on my breasts gaining a quicker, more insistent caress.

Faster now, he ups his speed and I gain eye contact with him. Harvey takes one hand from a breast and fists the hair at my temple. He yanks, sharp and shocking, and holds my head at an angle so I can't look at him.

Bastard.

With each plunge, his cock throbs, and he releases my other tit and slaps my right thigh, again, again, again. The blunt and wicked cracks against my skin entice my desires to the next level, and abruptly, he lets go of my hair and grabs my tit, his other hand still smacking.

"Faster, I'll fuck you faster."

His vast breaths, ragged, are cold as they sail towards me and hit my pubic hair.

I place my palms over his chest, run my fingers through his hairs, the crack-sting-crack of his hand striking my thigh heightening my pleasure. My core tightens, and my clit pulsates with such intensity I don't think I can hold off any longer.

I find his nipples with my fingers and once again make eye contact and flick-flick-flick his small, hard nubs with aggressiveness that borders on sadistic. He growls, slaps harder with less time between contact. My clit grinds against him, and an orgasm both inside and out races to completion.

The slaps stop, and he moves both of his hands to cup my shoulders. His nipples stand erect against my flicks, and as I'm almost at the point of no return, I grip them and twist, one way then the other. He grits his teeth and arches his back, rams into me — harder, faster...brutal movements that I love.

And it arrives. A burning simmers on low heat, gaining a gradually higher temperature with each plunge in, each bump against my cervix.

"Ah, shit, Princess. Fuck..."

Harvey closes his eyes, and his cock surges, seems to grow in girth. Its vein spasms inside me, his release imminent. He fists my hair again, wrenching my head to the side, and in a perverse act, I stare at him, pretending he stares at me, that he can look at me.

He jerks upward, and I scream through my orgasm, his hoarse yell joining my cries. My sweat-slicked legs slide against his outer thighs, and my tits bounce. The bittersweet pain of their movement brings tears to my eyes.

Spent, he flops over me—his exhalations fast, then slowing—and I snuggle my face into the crook of his neck. Once they regain their usual speed, I push his torso away and look at him.

Eyes still closed, he says, "As usual, fucking blinding," and pulls out of me, leaving me half on the beanbag, half off.

Charming, hmmm? I could be offended, but I'm not. He helps me as much as I help him. I'll be sated for a while now.

* * * *

12th June – Late afternoon

I didn't feel anything with Harvey, except, of course, the feelings that go with having sex. No love, no affection. I need that, can't keep going the way I am, fucking because I have to and not because I actually want to. But it's going to be difficult to find a man who can keep up with me. There's Shadow's client, the guy with the same problem as me. He'd be on hand whenever I wanted, but he doesn't particularly appeal to fuck on a regular basis. No, I need attraction, that deep-seated need inside me to share my life and secrets with a man, like Shadow has with Luke.

Will that day ever come?

My last client, number six, left around an hour ago. The stirrings of new desire already prod me to go in search of someone to give me relief. With Shadow out at Luke's most nights now, I can bring men home instead of fucking them down alleys or at their places. Maybe Shadow will move in with Luke, giving me free rein. I plan to go home, masturbate in the shower, then go out in search of some cock.

And maybe a bit of love to go with it.

Chapter Ten

Love?

I'm kidding myself if I think I'll find love here. Pubs are for meeting up with your friends or hooking up with guys for nothing more than what I need—a quick one-night stand that leaves you cold. Or hot, depending on the pace.

The Red Lion, a typical name for a typical British pub, leaves a lot to be desired. The décor is ancient— 1970s is my guess—and the furniture looks tired and worn, like it's seen too many arses, had too many hands touching it.

A bit like me, really.

I sit on a stool at the bar, positioned on the corner so I can see everyone coming and going. See any potential mates. I feel like a heel at times, a wanton slut out for what men can give me, but that's the way it's been ever since I became sexually active way too young to mention. Old friends—I say old, because they're not in my life any longer—shied away from me eventually, not wanting to be tarred with the same she's-a-whore brush, and who can blame them? I couldn't tell them what my problem was, that I can't help it. I doubt very much they'd have believed me anyway.

So now my only friend is Shadow, and Madam at a push. Maybe Shelley the receptionist. They understand what's going on with me. Well, they know. Might not understand, as such, but they accept me for who I am. I'm thankful for that, really I am, but if it weren't for Shadow and her complete faith in me that one day I'll find love, I don't know how I'd cope.

Nymphomania led me to the job I'm doing now. The only other alternative was becoming a prostitute of sorts, except I wouldn't have demanded payment. Standing on street corners or trawling the pathways of London in search of men wasn't, and still isn't, my cup of tea. Not that me visiting pubs and clubs for the same thing is any different. I'm still offering myself, still open to being used by men, still taking huge risks. I've been lucky so far and intend to remain that way. So long as I keep my wits about me, I should do okay.

The main door swings open, jarring me out of my thoughts. A guy enters, the type who looks as though he belongs to someone and has only nipped out for a quiet half pint before returning to the loving arms of his woman. Except...something's not right with him. He seems angry, what with his jerky body movements as he walks up to the bar and orders not a swift half but a shot of whisky.

A man with something on his mind.

Studying him isn't difficult. He's easy on the eyes, more so than any man I've seen lately, his cropped black hair gelled in place, his stubble giving him the rough-and-ready look I prefer. I imagine that stubble grazing over my folds, his tongue dipping inside me, lapping at my juices. The mental visual makes me squirm.

A small scar down the side of his face stretches from temple to jawbone. Did he get that in a fight or an accident? However it got there, it lends him a sexy-as-fuck air. By appearances alone, he's the kind of man I can see myself in bed with on a lazy Sunday morning, fucking before breakfast *and* after. And for the rest of the day. A woman would never get tired of him, with all that muscle and brawn on offer.

His black T-shirt fits him snugly, touching all the right places. A black belt through the waist loops of his dark blue jeans brings to mind me being whipped by it...or me whipping him, if that's what took his fancy.

I sit and wait, hoping it won't be long before he notices me and I can get eye contact. That's the deal breaker, the eyes. If I can engage men in a long stare, half the battle has been won.

He sips—and I'd thought he would have downed that drink in one go—gaze fixed on the bar top, frown firmly in place. Oh yes, he's troubled.

As though to save the barmaid the walk from the man to me, I slide off my stool and stand closer to the guy. Order a large glass of wine and seat myself beside him. He doesn't look to the side, just continues to stare at whatever he can see in his mind's eye. I wonder if a quick, anonymous fuck will make him feel better. It would me. My clit aches, and it won't be long before I soak my panties again.

I make a show of sipping my wine, the liquid ice cold as it goes down, condensation dripping onto my fingers. He doesn't flinch. My sighing doesn't grab his attention either. His glass being empty does. He orders a refill, and I smile at the sound of his voice, all rich tones and dulcet rumbles that would send a girl giddy if he spoke filthy talk against her cunt. New drink in hand, he stares at the bar again. Sips, sips, sips.

I'm clearly wasting my time.

I sigh again, making a move to leave his side.

"Don't go."

I stop and look at him, wondering what the hell's caused him to come here on his own. What woman in their right mind would want him going out by himself, for someone like me to hook their claws into? Sitting next to him again, I wait for him to speak. I'll give him another half hour, then I *have* to find someone else. I'm barely holding up here. The need for a fuck is too great.

Ten minutes go by, and still no word from him. My patience is running out.

"Look, if you just want someone to sit with, I'm not the woman for you." *That's a lie. I am, I want to be, but...* "I'm out tonight for reasons of my own, and sitting here in silence isn't one of them." I didn't mean to sound so harsh, but my nerves are raw...the bundle of nerves between my legs.

"I'm sick of this bollocks," he says, taking a larger sip of his drink than he has previously.

"Well, I am too, so I'll be seeing you." I act like I'm going to stand, to walk away.

He shoots his arm out, gripping my wrist, his touch hot, his hand large—big enough to cover one of my tits. The contact sets me off, clit buzzing, nipples hardening.

"Please, stay."

I settle back onto the stool, leaning slightly more to my left than I had before. Closer to him. "So, what's up? What bollocks are you sick of?"

I can't imagine being sick of bollocks.

He sighs. "This relationship lark. Getting it wrong all the time. Being too *needy*. That's what the last woman said I was anyway."

I wonder if this is his pick-up tactic, but something tells me he's genuinely at a loss. "Needy? In what way?"

"The usual. I want sex more than they do."

Thank the good Lord above. Has he sent me a man who likes sex more than three times a week? "Oh. Right. Some women don't like that, huh?"

"No, make that *all* women. In my experience anyway."

"You've hit the jackpot with me, mister. I'm so far removed from being all women you'll probably piss your pants in excitement if I tell you a little about myself." I clamp my mouth shut. I hadn't meant to say that out loud.

"Yeah, right. That's what they all say. I want a nice relationship as well as a good sex life. Is that too much to ask? I'm close to being thirty. All my mates are settled."

"Same here, but finding the right partner for the job is a pain up the bloody arse. I get that. God, do I get that. Okay, are you ready for me to talk?"

"Go ahead. What's one more lying woman added onto the list?"

"Hey!" I understand he's down in the dumps, but there's no need to cast me aside before he's even listened to what I have to say. "Don't assume I'm like the others. You have no idea what kind of woman I am." I stand abruptly, no longer wanting to help him out with a shoulder he can soak before walking away feeling better about himself after I've pumped his ego.

Suddenly I'm sick of bollocks after all.

"Wait!" he says, grabbing my wrist again. "I'm sorry. Talk to me."

Once again I sit. Once again my clit burns from his touch on my arm. "I'm a nymphomaniac." *That's it, just blurt it out.*

He snaps his head to the side so he's looking directly at me. The shock on his face makes me want to laugh, but I compose myself just in time. Giggling at his expression probably isn't a good idea. He's upset, lamenting the fact no woman can keep up with his demands. The last thing he needs is me laughing at him.

Try me on for size, gorgeous.

"Serious?" he asks, eyebrows rising over the deepest set of blues I've ever seen.

"Serious." I nod, sip some wine. "And it isn't all it's cracked up to be. I can't go long without sex. I work as a Domme in a sex dungeon just so I can get off more than once a day. I've tried relationships, and no man has been able to keep up with me. Fucking to get release, trying to even find men outside of work to fuck me hard and fast, isn't as easy as you might think. Women tend to get bad names for themselves if they like sex and go out to find it. Men...well, they just get called a stud, like it's okay for them to do it. *That's* bollocks." I sip again. Swallow. "As is being unable to find love because sex gets in the way. I scare men off."

"It's not just the sex for me, I swear it," he says. "I want the whole thing, the real deal. But, like you, I scare people away."

He laughs then, full throttle, head thrown back, the lot.

I wait for him to finish.

"Fucking crazy," he says.

"What is?"

He shakes his head, as though unable to believe he's stumbled upon a woman like me. "Who'd have thought I'd come out tonight and meet a woman who actually likes to fuck…a lot?"

"Who'd have thought I'd come out tonight and find a man who likes to fuck—a lot—and who also wants a loving relationship?"

"Like I said, crazy."

"But in a good way, right?"

"Yeah. So…?"

"Yes, I'm up for it, but the funny thing is, even though I could do with a balls-slapping-my-arsehole fuck, I don't want to do that with you. Not tonight. Not if something else could come out of it, too."

"Just my luck." He smiles sadly.

"That's probably not what you wanted to hear, but despite me needing that fuck, I also need love. Cheesy and contradictory, I know."

He shakes his head. "Not really. We all need that."

His closeness is driving me insane. The fact that I'm not dragging him out of here by his ear, pushing him up against a wall, and instructing him to shove his hard cock into my cunt is driving me more so.

"I just need to visit the toilet," I say.

"Yep, and then I'll never see you again. I know the drill."

"Listen." I leave my stool and stand behind him, pressing my tits against his back. "When I say I'm just visiting the toilet, that's exactly what I'm doing. The reason I'm going there isn't what you think. I *have* to go in there for some *privacy*. Do you understand what I'm saying?"

He turns his head to the side, tries to look at me over his shoulder. "Fuck. That is a major turn-on."

"Yes, well, you just sit there and imagine what I'm doing. There's something about you, and I don't even know your bloody name. I don't want to mess up any chance I have with you. Okay?"

He nods, grips his glass so hard his knuckles turn white.

"I'm going to masturbate," I whisper, "and think of you."

His sharp intake of breath fills my ears as I push off him and saunter towards the ladies' room.

His shout of "My name's Ben!" makes me smile so hard my face hurts.

* * * *

I return to his side, and he glances at me, cheeks a little red, hands dangling between his legs. I stare at them, then back at his face.

"I had to hide..." He nods at his hands. "You know."

"Yeah, I know. Take my hand."

He does.

"Kiss my fingers."

He lifts my hand to his lips, his eyes going wide. "Jesus fuck, I can smell you."

"I didn't wash them. Taste them, if you want."

He swallows, Adam's apple bobbing. "My God, what the hell have I stumbled on here?"

"The love of your life, mister, if you play your cards right." I sounded bold then, sure of myself, but I've had to learn to be that way. To get what I need.

He opens his mouth, top lip undeniably cute and full, and sucks one of my fingers inside. He groans, despite the barmaid hovering nearby, and looks into my eyes.

God, I want him.

"Taste good?"

He nods, swirls his tongue around my finger, then eases it out of his mouth. "Too fucking good. And you are too good to be true. There's got to be a catch."

"No catch. Like I said, I need a lot of sex. I want you, I won't deny it, but I'm also like any other regular woman. I want to be dated, made to feel special. You up for that?"

"Damn right I am." He kisses my fingers then licks his lips. Closes his eyes a little. "Fuck, you're hot."

"And I'll get a whole lot hotter before this week is out. I want to be clear on something, though."

"What's that?"

"Until you fuck me, I'm going to do my job like I've always done it. I won't fuck anyone outside of work hours, because if you want, we'll be together every night." I smile. "You'll be taking me out, wining and dining me, being the perfect gentleman. But the minute we have sex, everyone else goes out the window. If you can keep up with me for the most part, then I can masturbate the other times I get the urge."

"Shit. You're killing me." He glances at his groin again.

"Poor baby. Think you can wait until Friday to get into my panties?"

"I'll have to, won't I?" He pauses, looking at me and shaking his head. "Seriously now, are you for real?"

"Yep. So, give me your number, your address."

He pulls a mobile out of his pocket, and I add his information to mine. I stand, throw the rest of my wine down my throat, and lean in close, my lips millimetres from his.

"Tomorrow night. Here. Seven o'clock. Then we'll decide where you're taking me."

He nods, the eye contact between us searing.

I back away towards the door and, just before I disappear into the night I say, "And my name's Klara Woods."

Chapter Eleven

Trois
13ᵗʰ June – Morning

Last night panned out as I had hoped in the love stakes, but not with my desires not being met. I went home after leaving Ben, masturbating wildly in bed, bringing his face to mind, the feel of his hand on my wrist. The way he looked at me with those blue eyes of his. God, I'd come harder than I had in a long time.

I didn't masturbate before work again this morning. Difficult not to, but I succeeded. I have a double-client session – Mark and Gregg, friends who visit me for a threesome once a month. Our meetings are always explosive, so after I've closed this entry, I'll ready myself in the outfit of their choice – the policewoman's uniform.

Those naughty boys. You'd think they'd be sick of seeing the navy blue of the law.

While they fuck me, I'll imagine they're Ben.

Name: Mark Sampson & Gregg Tripp
Preference: Mark – baton slaps, handcuffs. Gregg – face slaps, degrading talk.
Notes: Mark and Gregg enjoy acting out the scenario of being arrested and taken to a cell, where a female officer overcomes them with her dominance and sexual prowess.

I enter my dungeon, pleased to find Madam had the red leather bed removed and the huge cage erected in its place. Today, I'll be entertaining all clients who prefer the iron-barred room. It saves too much shifting of furniture in between sessions.

A hard wooden bench, an itchy grey blanket on top of it, sits inside the cage to the left, and a fake toilet occupies the far right corner. A small wooden table, between the bench and the toilet, holds a loo roll and a paperback book. Authenticity promotes a more risqué session, but I draw the line at the aroma of urine. The usual light shines brighter, replaced by a hundred-watt bulb casting its stark beam on the walls and the instruments. The steel of handcuffs, chains, and some whip handles glint, almost winking at me as if to entice me to use them.

In my changing room, I shirk off my jeans, baggy T-shirt, sports bra, comfortable panties, and open the wardrobe. All outfits hang beneath transparent packaging, the PVC and rubber wiped clean after I leave, the fabrics dry-cleaned overnight. WPC Darkness is about to be born once again. I love being her, especially with Mark and Gregg. Two cocks in one session. Who's complaining?

I wonder if Ben likes dress-up scenarios. Whether he'll enjoy fucking my cunt while a baton fucks my arse? Time will tell whether he's up for anything like that.

Thank goodness the material of this uniform doesn't scratch. The skirt, shorter than the average WPC's, is just long enough to cover my bottom. The jacket's hem rests a couple of inches above that, the tight belt accentuating my slim waist. No blouse beneath it, though I do wear a black-and-white checked tie with a Velcro neckband.

A double-fisted rap shakes the door—they always insist on both knocking—and I say, "Come in!"

The men enter, bringing with them the scent of the outdoors, a jostle of bodies as though they've been shoved inside from behind. All part of the play.

"Thank you, Sergeant," I say to the non-existent policeman and glare at the miscreants one at a time.

Gregg, his head of black hair a halo of tight curls, his cheeks ruddy and sun-warmed, puffs out his chest in a typical criminal's defiance. He jams his hands on his hips. Already, small sweat rings on his white T-shirt beneath his arms indicate the heat of desire. In a silent prayer, I thank Madam for the air conditioning. His denims, strategically ripped on the knees and thighs, enhance his muscled legs. Sprinkles of black leg hair peep through the slits, and I clench my cunt, warn myself not to launch into the throes of exhilaration too soon.

"You again, Mr Tripp? Can't seem to stay out of trouble, can you?"

He nods, blue eyes wide, and smirks, uncaring of the misdemeanours that bring him here.

Mark closes the door with a tanned hand, his wide forearms covered in blond downy hair. He stares at me, green eyes penetrative, and I long for the session to fast-forward so he can penetrate me with something else entirely. His black vest boasts the slogan in white—'HOT AS FUCK'. I imagine people take that to mean the weather when he wears it in the summer.

He's taller than Gregg by a couple of inches, putting him around six feet. Mark's appearance garners respect. Long legs and a muscled torso showcase his compulsion to work out. He clenches his fists, and his biceps bulge.

"And you, Mark. I'm not surprised in the slightest that you're here again. It seems neither of you can stay on the right side of the law." I pull a small notepad from my jacket pocket and remove the pencil from the spirals. "All possessions on the table by the door. Now."

The men glare, and a minute smile tickles my lips. Gregg empties his pockets and throws his payment, a wallet, and a set of car keys on the table.

I step towards him and slap his face, the resounding noise a portent of what's to come. I jot down his belongings in my book. "Take off your watch and go into the changing room, felon. Strip, and don't come out until naked."

He clenches his jaw and struts past me, eyes dark and foreboding. The *schlink* of the changing room curtain rings gives evidence of his anger and inability to accept the slap, despite him asking for it in his initial interview with Madam.

Mark tosses his payment, a wallet, and a fifty-pence piece on the table. He nods at the coin. "Just about all you're worth, pig," he says, his voice hard, disdain-filled, but his eyes show me he's lying.

I whip the baton from my uniform belt and crack him on the back of his thigh. My nose almost touching his, our eyes boring into one another's, I whisper, "Don't fuck with me, thief. My baton has a tendency to give harsher pain the more you piss me off."

His sneer of pleasure ignites excitement in my belly. I shove the baton into its slot on my waist, look away, down at my notebook, and scribble the contents of his pockets on the page.

"Do as the other was instructed. No longer than five minutes." I snap my notebook closed, turn from him, and place it on the steel table between two Tupperware boxes containing condoms and lube.

A swish of displaced air caresses my legs, and his footsteps tromp past. The curtain rustles, as do their voices. Though lowered, their conversation sails out to me.

"Fuck, she's harsh today." Mark, a little…bewildered?

"That's good. I want a rough session this morning. S'like she picks up on vibes or summat." Gregg, as perceptive as ever.

"Bloody adore her, I do."

Oh. Well. I didn't expect that. Them caring.

The backs of my eyes sting, and I inhale deep, switch my emotions off, and walk over to the left wall. "You'd better be undressed, boys. Get the hell out here *now*!"

The hardmen, who spend their days collecting payoffs, frightening small-time crooks off their patch, and securing the respect of many, step out of the changing room. Cocks stiff, muscles bunched, scowls on their faces. From where I stand, it already looks as though they're in the cage.

"Step over here." I select two pairs of handcuffs and stand at the cage door. "Inside." I flick my gaze from them to the cell's interior, and they do as I bade. I follow and close the door. "You" — I point at Mark — "move the table. Stand between the bench and the toilet, facing me. Star-shaped, arms above your head."

Mark hesitates at the deviation from our usual scenario. His beautiful cock sways a little, his arse cheeks tight.

"Move! Arms wider. Grip the bars."

He complies, and I snap a handcuff on each wrist, securing the other ends to the cage. He releases a quick breath, and his prick jolts. I match my position to his, cover his hands with mine, and press myself against him. The heat of his erection penetrates my lower abdomen.

"Mmmm." I grab my baton. "Hot as fuck, eh?"

The baton bites his other thigh, and he screws his eyes closed, breathes through his nose, whispers upon exhalation, "Bitch pig."

"Ah," I whisper against his lips, "but you love it."

I'm wet, and the urge to impale myself on his cock is almost too much to endure. "And you" — I turn to Gregg and replace my baton — "come here."

It takes two paces for him to reach me and receive a stinging blow to his cheek, the other still bearing an angry red handprint. He widens his eyes, and before he fully registers my action, I slap him again.

I select my baton once more. "Take off my jacket, felon."

Gregg frowns but unbuttons it, head down. His fingers shake, and I look at Mark, lick my lips, and move my gaze to Gregg's cock. An average size, but fuck, does he use it well. I recall times past when this man's dick has hit the spot immediately, and my cunt clenches.

Mustn't come now. Not until the main event.

Gregg slips my jacket off my shoulders, the whisper of fabric a melody to accompany their percussive breaths. Mark groans at the sight of my tits, and the handcuff chains tinkle. Poor boy wants to touch. Gregg forms his hands into fists.

"Remove my tie," I say.

I stare at Gregg. How he longs to disobey. His nature screams for him to do so, yet he reaches out and rips the Velcro apart, throwing the garment to the bench behind me.

"Touch my tits, gangster. Rub my nipples...hard."

Another groan from Mark, and Gregg covers my breasts with his hands, kneading their fullness. He smoothes his fingertips over his palms' previous path and finds my erect nipples. He pinches, and Mark runs his foot up and down my leg. His pained vocals and my aching clit alert me to the time. I must move on.

I take two condoms from my jacket pocket and hand one to Gregg. "Pick it up and put it on." The other, I remove from the packet, face Mark, and bend over so my bare arse is on show for Gregg's steely gaze. The crackle of rubber as Gregg covers his cock blends with the sound of me rolling the condom down Mark's shaft. I kneel in front of Mark and look up at him. His cheeks flush, and he fists his hands.

"I'm going to suck you," I whisper to Mark, then to Gregg, "And you—on your knees behind me. Do *not* touch me yet."

I swirl my tongue around the head of Mark's dick and palm his shaft, moving my hand up and down. He draws in a sharp breath, and I imagine he watches my lips envelop his tip. The vein throbs, and I take him deep, my tongue pressed against his length from bottom to top, bottom to top, over and over.

At the head again, I rest it on my bottom lip and command Gregg, "You behind me. Get inside me. Now."

I resume my ministrations to Mark's cock, and Gregg's warm hands encircle my waist. I slide my knees further apart to accommodate him between my legs and jut out my arse. Gregg slips inside my wetness and pumps—frantic, hard. He moves his hands down and grips my hips—as usual, taking what he wants, his own enjoyment paramount.

Mark's cock twitches, and I take it out of my mouth, straighten my torso. Cock in my hand, I masturbate him, his tip between my cleavage, and revel in the sensations Gregg's dick produces in my cunt. My clit throbs to the same beat as Mark's vein, Gregg's movements, and I stare up at Mark, making eye contact. His fists and jaw clenched, his wrists straining against the handcuffs, unleashes the sensation that Gregg's cock is a blade of fire in my core.

"Faster…harder, felon!"

Mark's abdomen arches forward, and his hot cum spurts into the condom. Gregg pants, groans, and thrusts once, twice, and judders against my arse. A roar of ecstasy leaves my mouth, and a wave of pleasure radiates from my clit and G-spot.

"Ah, fuck. Fuck, yes!" I cry, eyes closed, head thrown back.

Our gasps fly from us out of sync, a cacophony of hoarse exhalations.

I'm already up for more. "Time to switch."

Gregg eases out of me. I release Mark's cock and lean over to my jacket, take out wet wipe sachets and hand them to the men. The handcuff key follows, and I free Mark's wrists. He rubs them and washes himself, semi-hard, for he knows act two is imminent. Two more condoms, one given to Mark, the other on the floor beside me, herald a repeat performance, though the actors switch places. Gregg winces at the tightness of the handcuffs, and Mark, to the side of me, masturbates himself hard again.

I stare into Gregg's eyes. "Ready?"

He nods and plants his feet further apart.

The previous scene repeats, though Mark inside me is a little less rough, a little less selfish. He rubs my breasts, a sensuous, caring action, and his thrusts border on a lover's. Gregg pushes himself further into my mouth, his hardness increasing with each suck, each glide up and down his cock. Impatient.

Mark curves over me, his front warm on my back, and whispers, "You're beautiful. I love you," all the while his hands delicate on my breasts.

His endearment spurs on a fresh orgasm inside me, and I hold Gregg's cock upwards so his cock doesn't touch me, doesn't sully the splendour of Mark's caress. I chase the thrill, revel in Mark's attentions, and imagine…imagine… Ben.

An orgasm, sharp, so beautiful, eclipses any other I have felt with a man. Mark's *aah* of release spawns warmth in my belly, quickly doused by Gregg's jubilant, aggressive shout.

Session over, I tap Mark's right thigh, and he slips out, stands up. I, too, stand and unlock Gregg's wrists then throw the handcuffs to the bench. Their landing clank jolts me out of my reverie, chases the questions forming in my mind. I mustn't get attached, despite Mark's declaration of love. He doesn't mean it.

While the men wash and dress in their changing room, I do the same in mine.

All of us back in the dungeon, Gregg opens the door and steps into the hallway, hands in pockets. Mark loiters beside the cage. He looks at me, as I do him, and something passes between us, an unspoken understanding.

He leans into me and whispers, "I'll visit you on my own. Soon." He brushes my cheek with his fingertips, my jawline, my neck, and I clasp his hand to stop their journey going further south. He smiles, a bittersweet curve of his lips, and leaves the room in reverse, closing the door with a pain-filled expression.

How did I miss that before? How did I not see how he feels about me?

Chapter Twelve

The First Date

I'm not really sure how to dress. I have no idea where Ben will take me — or if he's even going to show up. I'm sure he will, but doubt always creeps in, doesn't it? I ferret through the clothes hanging in my wardrobe, feeling the fabrics to get an idea how they'll feel to Ben if he touches them. Settling on a little black dress, silk and very sexy, coupled with a pair of high-heeled black patents, I'm happy with how I look. Blonde hair always looks good against black clothing, so a man once told me.

Nerves dancing in my belly, I climb into the taxi outside our apartment. I don't want to stick to just one alcoholic drink tonight. As the car speeds away and into the city proper, I think about earlier and what Mark had said. He hadn't meant it, surely. He's never said anything like that before, and it makes me wonder if men can sense when a woman has another on her mind. Does their testosterone level go up when a woman they find attractive is seeing someone else? I suspect that's true and put his words down to that. And if he is interested and things work out with Ben? Well, that's just tough. Mark will just have to accept he missed the boat.

I feel cruel thinking that, sound very mean, but something about Ben ticks all my boxes, even though I hardly know him. I wouldn't call it love at first sight...more like attraction on various levels. The vulnerability he displayed when he'd opened up so quickly, obviously desperate to get things off his chest. The way he was able to tell me he wanted love as well as sex—how many men would admit to that on the first meeting? I like that. It shows he's in touch with his feminine side, or that he knows what he wants and isn't afraid to say so. I imagine that trait will serve him well.

And me, if I end up in his future.

I look out of the taxi window and watch the world go by. House lights draw me, and I wonder what people are doing behind those closed front doors. One day I hope to live in a house and not an apartment, with a husband and children, maybe a dog or cat to make the family complete. And I'd have a regular job. I can't see that happening right now, but perhaps, given time, my homey fantasy will come true. It would be nice, wouldn't it?

At The Red Lion, I climb out of the taxi, pay the fare to the leering driver, whose gaze is directly on my cleavage, and for once shudder at the attention. This time forty-eight hours ago I'd have asked him if he fancied a quickie on his back seat, uncaring what he looks like.

How fast things change.

I walk away, uncomfortable knowing he's following my every move, thinking of whipping around to face him and asking if he wants to take a picture. Seeing his mouth drop open, maybe a lurid retort coming from it, a denial that he even wants to fuck me anyway. Some men are such arseholes, aren't they?

Still, I refuse to buckle under the pressure and instead push into the pub. It's crowded tonight, compared to last. I see the reason why. A pub quiz is in full swing. I look out of place among the casually dressed crowd, most of them wearing jeans and sweaters or T-shirts emblazoned with some comment or other. It brings Mark to mind again, and I shove thoughts of him away. I don't want to entertain images of him. Not when Ben, God bless him, sits at the bar where he sat last night.

I could kiss him senseless just for turning up.

Tonight he's dressed to impress. No taking a woman for granted with this man. He hasn't lost the will to make an effort despite what he's been through with other women, and it makes me feel special, like I'm worth bothering for. Like I matter.

A black suit covers him nicely, stretched tantalisingly across his back and shoulders, the hem riding up to show the beautiful swell of his arse against the stool. The suit looks like one from off the rack, although I'd say it still cost a pretty penny. Not that it matters.

My cunt spasms as I contemplate walking up behind him, roving my hands over those delectable swells, then snaking my hands around the front to feel his cock harden beneath my palms.

Stop it. You're only going to end up uncomfortable in the pussy department if you keep thinking like that.

I can't help it, though, and as I make my way towards him, more dirty thoughts prance through my head. Ben sucking my nipples. Ben's rock hard dick shoving into me. Ben's hands all over me, everywhere at once. Fingers on my nipples—pinching, pulling. Fingers sliding up and down my slit, the tip of one circling my swelling bud. Ben gazing into my eyes as he shoots his load, with that feral look men get taking over his face, his thrusts more forceful as he strives to empty his bollocks, loosing cum into my ever-needy cunt. His breaths growing ragged—him grinding out that, fuck, I'm a sexy bitch who drives him insane and he loves, loves, loves me. Wants this forever—*me* forever.

I slide onto the empty stool next to his and press my thighs together, clench my cunt muscles to stave off the need to come. "Hey."

He turns to stare at me, widening his eyes as he looks me up and down, gaze coming to rest on my face. "Aww, fuck. You're beautiful."

"You don't scrub up so bad yourself. How's it hanging?" I glance between his legs.

"It was hanging fine until you came along. Now it's standing."

"I can see that."

"D'you want a drink in here, or shall we get going?"

"Get going. I'm curious as to what you have planned."

He downs the rest of his lager—only an inch or so left in the glass—and stands, holding his arms out. "Just a small hug, that's all I want."

I step into his embrace, his arms encompassing me, and all at once feel safe, wanted and desired. His erection presses into my lower belly, and I glance up at him, into those blue eyes that I know will haunt me forever if things go wrong and I don't see them again.

He leans down, whispers in my ear, "Fuck, I could explode right now, in front of all these people. You're that hot."

I stand on tiptoe and brush my lips across his cheek. "I could come myself, could go into the ladies' for some privacy before we leave, but I'm not going to."

He pulls back, looking down at me, a wicked smile on his lips. "Do you *need* to visit the toilet before we leave?"

I slap his chest gently. "Yes, I bloody well do, but like I said, I won't."

"Shame. I wanted to do a bit of imagining. A bit of tasting after."

"Well, you can't. Having me with you in person will have to do instead."

He positions his suit jacket over his bulge, leads me outside by the hand and tugs me along the street.

"Where are we going?" I ask, my heels clacking on the pavement.

"Just down the road a bit. It isn't far."

"We're eating?"

"Too right we're eating."

"Not each other, I hope. Not tonight, anyway."

"Fuck."

I laugh and decide I might renege on that one. I'll see how things go.

The joy of the night seeps into me. Other couples and groups of friends pour out of pubs along the way, their chatter and laughter disappearing when they enter the next place on their list. Ben hugs me to him, his arm tight about my back, hand fitting nicely in the curve of my waist. We talk about his day, and how him being a plumber can sometimes be a nightmare on his social life if he's on twenty-four-hour call. This feels so good I want to shout out and let everyone know I'm on a date—a real one, where sex won't end the night, where a guy is taking me out and being a gentleman. Albeit a gentleman with filthy thoughts, but still…

"Come on, you," Ben says, "we're going in here."

He pushes open the heavy glass door of Helden's, a posh eatery I've only ever been to once with a rich client who insisted I meet him for dinner and act as his escort for the night. I hadn't complained. He paid me well, with cash and sex, and he'd been easy to entertain. I just had to laugh a lot, look pretty, and make him come harder than he had in his entire life.

The tricks of my trade had come in handy that night.

Inside Helden's, seated and with our orders scribbled on a notepad by a harassed-looking waiter, Ben pours white wine and settles back in his chair opposite mine. He studies me, his pose languid, one elbow resting on his chair arm. With two fingers and his thumb, he toys with his lower lip. I want to lick that lip, to suck it gently, swirling my tongue over it until he moans. I want to get up, go over and straddle him, press my cunt to his erection, let him know how much I want him. I want everyone here to disappear. I wish we were alone so I can go back on my word and watch as he strips my clothes off, see his reaction to my naked body. See if it's everything he's imagined. Hope it's more. I want to experience that first hot touch of skin on skin that sets my nerve endings on fire, my cunt on fire.

My clit pulsates.

Shit.

"I need the toilet," I blurt.

"Jesus. This isn't the right place, kitten."

Kitten? I decide I quite like that and smile. "It doesn't matter where I am. If I need privacy, I need privacy. I don't think you quite get the full extent of my need."

"I don't, but I plan on sticking around to find out."

"Come with me. Watch me."

"What?" He shoots forward, hands on his knees.

"You heard me."

"I did, but you said—"

"I said we wouldn't fuck each other until Friday. It doesn't mean you can't watch while I fuck myself."

Ben glances around nervously. "I can't just go into the ladies' room."

"Why not?"

"I'll get kicked out of here if I'm caught."

"So?"

"Fucking hell…"

I walk away, knowing damn well he'll follow.

"Our meals," he calls. "What about them?"

I ignore him and head for the restrooms. Once through the main door, I wait in a square, carpeted lobby with three doors that lead to the toilets—men's, women's and disabled. I wait for him to join me. Right on cue, he does, appearing in a flurry of breaths and cool air. He's so fucking hot I could shag him right here, right now.

Instead, I enter the ladies' room, glancing left then right. "Clear." I walk inside, hearing Ben's footsteps behind me, and make my way over to one of the wider stalls at the end of a row. I go inside, beckon for him to join me, then lock the door when we're both sandwiched inside.

"Ready?" I ask.

"Fuck no. I mean yes. Shit, I've never done anything like this before."

I press myself to the cubicle wall and hike up my dress, exposing my wet cunt. "First time for everything." I dip two fingers into my slit. "And like I said last night, you've hit the jackpot with me, mister."

He leans on the door, hands splayed against it either side of him, his breathing uneven. "No underwear. Jesus, woman! This is nuts."

I swirl my fingers around my clit. "But fucking hot. Look."

He glances down. "Christ, yes."

I watch him watching me. His gaze is riveted to my busy fingers, and a gush of juices flood my folds. I push my fingers inside to scoop the cream, slathering it over my clit. He's rapt, one hand straying to the bulge in his trousers.

"Fuck, I want to touch you," he grinds out.

"You...can't. I'm nearly...there."

"So fast? Jesus Christ, you're driving me crazy."

A flushing toilet and the squeak of hinges heightens my need.

"Shit!" he whispers. "Someone's in here!"

I climax, closing my eyes, releasing little whimpers. Bliss pours into me, my labia swelling right along with my clit. My body jerks, back slapping against the wall, and I moan through my release, uncaring who the hell hears.

"Be quiet, kitten. Please... Fuck, this is so bad."

As the pleasure recedes, I open my eyes to find Ben stroking his bulge. "Stop it. No touching yourself allowed."

He jerks his hand away, staring at me as though he wants to lunge forward and kiss me. "That how you talk to your clients? Like that? All bossy?"

"You haven't heard anything yet, mister."

I shimmy down my dress and take one step forward, settling myself against him. "Hungry?"

He looks down at my hand and nods.

"Good. I expect our meals are ready by now." I pat his thigh to make him move out of the way.

"Wait! You asked if I was hungry," he says, shuffling aside.

I unlock the door and open it enough that I can slip through the gap. "And like I said, our meals will be ready. Whatever did you think I meant?" I wink and saunter over to the sink to wash my hands, lifting my head so I can look in the mirror and see him in the stall behind me.

"You're washing it off, you teasing little — "

"But you love it. Don't you?" I ask.

"Hell yes, but — "

"But nothing. Come on. I'd hate for our food to get cold."

* * * *

The food tasted wonderful. I had steak with duchesse potatoes and minted peas. Ben chose the same, except he had thick-cut fries. Now, we wait for dessert — an ice cream delight big enough to share. The harried waiter returns to our table and places the cold confection between us and hands out two long spoons.

"Enjoy," he says. "And good luck finishing it."

I can see what he means. The amount of ice cream, chocolate fudge cake chunks, whipped cream and chocolate swirls is enough to feed four people. I dig my spoon into the cream, scoop up a big blob, then place cream on my side plate. Ben looks at me curiously.

I let my napkin flutter beneath the table. "Oh, I appear to have dropped something." Pushing my chair back, I crawl under the table, reposition the hanging side of the tablecloth, and undo Ben's fly.

"What the hell are you doing?" he hisses. "Someone will see you!"

"I won't be under here long enough for anyone to know what I'm doing."

"You said we wouldn't fuck until Friday."

"And we won't. Tonight is just a lick, I promise. Friday is the real deal. The full-on treatment."

"You said you wanted to just be wined and dined."

"I changed my mind."

"This is… God, this is a first for me. Klara, stop it. We'll get caught."

I free his cock then reach my hand up to feel for my side plate. Finding it, I bring it under the table, tip it on its side, and watch the cream slide off and onto his cock.

He groans quietly. "Christ Almighty, that's cold!"

Plate on the floor, my fingers curled around the base of his cock, I shuffle between his legs and lick my lips.

"Ready?" I ask.

"Yes. No. Wait…"

I plunge his cock into my mouth, cream dripping down my chin. Ben's moan is barely audible, but I hear it just the same. His cock pulses against my curled tongue, and I draw upwards, ultra slowly, swallowing the cream and wishing it was a different kind altogether. Another dip of my head, another hard, slow suck on his length, one more dip for good measure, and I pull upwards again, letting his dick pop out of my mouth. I want to suck him until he comes, but the location isn't the best of places to do that. Besides, a little teaser won't hurt him. I let his cock go, pick up the plate, and retake my seat. I stare across the table at him, wiping my chin with a napkin, noting his flushed cheeks and pained expression.

"That was so cruel," he says, hands disappearing to tuck his erection away. "So cruel."

"But you love this, right? The thrill. The danger."

"Yes, but—"

"Then being in a relationship with me will suit you just fine. Ice cream, Ben?"

I dig my spoon into the goo and slide some into my mouth.

"You're wicked." His cheeks are a darker shade of red now.

"I know."

"I wanted you to make me come."

"I know that, too."

He leans forward, looking left to right then back at me. Says quietly, "Did you want to come? To make me come?"

"Fuck, yes."

He shakes his head. "Where the hell have you been all my life?"

"Struggling to find someone like you."

It's as open as I'm prepared to be at the moment. There's enough time for baring souls another night. This evening is all about showing him how far I'm prepared to go to sate our needs. That I'm not the kind of woman who shirks sex and will leave him wanting. Well…I've left him wanting, but in a good way. He'll be so fired up by Friday he'll be ready to take what I'm thinking of dishing out.

Ben's gaze turns soft, and his features go slack. He cocks his head, regarding me with such a wonderful stare that I'm hard pressed not to melt.

"I'm already falling in love with you, kitten, you need to know that before we go any further."

"You are?" God, that was quick. It's what I want, but I'm still shocked.

He nods, picking up his spoon and playing with it. "I couldn't stop thinking about you last night. Or today. Couldn't wait to meet you again. For the first time I can really see me getting along with a woman in all respects. It's…what you just did, in the toilet, under the table. I've wanted a woman like you." He squeezes his chin between thumb and finger. "And your job. Christ, the things you must know."

"Oh, I know a lot, Ben. Maybe you'd like me to show you sometime."

"Maybe? There's no maybe about it."

Chapter Thirteen

Marked
14th June – Morning

With Ben on my mind, I arrived home last night and bathed, once again fondling myself to completion with thoughts of him gliding through my mind. I left the bathroom wrapped in a pink towelling robe. Shadow was home, and she frowned, cocking her head as though sensing something different about me. I haven't told her about Ben yet. I won't until after Friday. What if our weeknight dates prove we had nothing in common but the need for sex and love? If I keep acting as I did last night, I'll never find out. I'd slipped into my usual pattern, I know that, so tonight I won't do it. Tonight we'll talk and get to know one another a little better.

But what if Ben doesn't like what he finds?

I'm in turmoil, with no idea how to cope with these newfound feelings. I haven't allowed myself to warm to any man for months, yet Ben has torn down my defences and unleashed a flurry of questions I don't know how to answer.

Do I feel anything for him? Anything real? Something I can hold on to and build on?

I think so. Or maybe I'm afraid to admit I do because a dream like this coming true then going tits up is likely to hurt...too much.

Apart from the chat before we went into Helden's and the conversation about everything and nothing after dessert, last night was just like any of the others I've participated in. Me being the cock tease, the man under my spell. The only difference being the evening hadn't ended with us tangled in one another's arms, cocks and tongues probing, but a lot of the conversation had revolved around sex, innuendoes flying.

To top it all, Madam has sent me a new client this morning with his information sheet blank. She didn't have time to fill one out, apparently.

I so hate working off the cuff. And if it wasn't for the raging desire inside me, I wouldn't work today at all.

```
Name: Unknown new client
Preference: Unknown
Notes: None as yet.
```

My mind unfocused on the job at hand, I stare at the clothing in my dressing room wardrobe. What should I choose without knowing the client's preferences? Should I play it safe and wear the plain, black rubber dress, or take a risk and pick out a themed costume? No. Themed may prove disastrous. The nun's outfit would freak out a priest, and nurses' attire would possibly bore a doctor, should the new client be either of those.

The dress my safest bet, I disrobe and put it on, my cunt willing but my mind not playing ball. Inhaling a gulp of air and fortitude, about to slip my feet into a pair of black stilettos, I jump at the sound of a knock on the door. The client, a little early—or maybe Madam has garnered some information about the man after all and wants to let me know before he arrives?

Barefoot, I leave my dressing room, conscious that no makeup pretties my face, that no brush has tidied my hair from its present messy ponytail into a beautiful, loose mane. The red walls of my dungeon appear closer than usual, the ceiling light duller, the red leather bed somehow less spotlit beneath the central bulb. That my state of mind affects my surroundings gives me a good indication that Ben's revelation about falling in love with me has rocked my equilibrium more than I'd thought.

Instead of calling for the guest to enter, I open the door and peer around its edge, ready to ask the client to give me five minutes or to take the sheet of notes from Madam.

Mark stands in the hallway, hands in his pockets, looking at me from beneath lowered lashes. A sheepish grin touches his lips, and a blush stains his cheeks and chin. He kicks the air as though displacing an errant pebble in a cobblestone street. I should have known, should have guessed he could persuade Madam to let him visit me with no information on him whatsoever. He's taken the choice from me, arrived so that I have to deal with his admission and not shelve it like I had planned to do, keeping it how it was before with him only visiting with Gregg. So much easier. Less complicated.

"Oh! It's you." Funny how we state the obvious at times like this.

"Yes." He kicks the 'pebble' again. "It's me. Do you mind?"

I grip the edge of the door and step back. It doesn't matter if I do mind, does it? Yes, I could turn him away, explain to Madam that Mark is getting a bit too…close, but there's no guarantee another Domme is available to fuck him…and it seems he doesn't want anyone else anyway. If me going to Madam means her losing a customer because I've refused to deal with him, she won't be as friendly as usual. I've seen her turn nasty and don't fancy being on the end of her temper. If you do as you're told, she's wonderful. I'd like to keep our relationship that way.

"No, no," I lie. "Let me just go and get changed again. But you won't be able to have the cage. I didn't know in advance that you —"

"Don't want the cage or uniform. Just you." He strides past me into the dungeon.

My stomach clenches. What does he mean? Just me, as in, an ordinary fuck today, or...? The thought of Ben comes to mind, he of the sexy body, the gorgeous mouth. He owns a piece of my heart that I'm sure I can't rent out to this man, too. Not now.

I told myself long ago I wasn't in anything for the long haul. I only allowed tenants. I was the landlady who ruled her domain with a steady heartbeat. If the heartbeat flickered just one throb out of place when dealing with — with what, love? — then it would wreck my well-constructed shield.

Until I met Ben.

I close the door, lean against it, and stare at Mark, who has thrown my emotions into confusion. Love? How can he love me? How can he even care about me? I can deal with infatuation — all the clients have a touch of that — but a proper relationship, no. Okay, Shadow and Luke managed it, but they were the exception. I'd been capable of a proper relationship only once, but my insatiable desires had ruined it. With Ben, things might be so different.

Mark leans his arse against the bed end, grips its corners, legs crossed at the ankles. This criminal incites such a burning desire in me to fuck, and I marvel that I've kept my hands from removing his black polo shirt, his denims. I'll be using him — a vessel to sate my needs and nothing more. No emotions involved. No...emotions belong with Ben.

I move towards Mark and, legs apart, mould my body against his. My face inches from his, I look into his eyes, which show such adoration that I have to force myself to believe it's lust and nothing more.

I don't want this crap. Can't deal with it. Not now. Just let us fuck, that's all I want. All I need.

"Touch me," I whisper and lean forward, tracing my tongue along his full bottom lip, eye contact still maintained.

He roams my back, the contours of my arse with confident hands, and I palm his chest—the feel of his shirt soft, the scent of his aftershave, his personal aroma, a miasma sent to entice me into his web. I'll fuck him and fuck him good, but anything else, forget it.

"You do realise," I say, "that this is the only way you'll get a part of me."

With soft lips, he brushes my lips, my jawline, my neck. "I thought maybe—"

I hang my head back, savour the tingles his mouth brings, and clutch his pecs. "You're not listening to me. What did I just say?"

He sighs, his exhalation hot on my skin, and emotion must grip him—he crushes me harder against his body, and his kisses grow more insistent, more lust-fuelled.

"I... Fuck, I'm in love with you, Darkness." He trails a path with his tongue from my ear to my collarbone. "Can't stop thinking about you. I get jealous when I share you with Gregg. I want you all to myself. For you to give up this job, be with me all the time."

I smile, a sorrowful twitch of the lips, and understand the situation for what it is now. His visit, an epiphany, releases all pressures from my mind and body. "No, you're in love with the idea of who I am. In love with the person I present to you. I'm not that person."

I close my eyes, press my groin into his, and gyrate a figure of eight. His thigh muscles and cock tauten, as do his fingers on my arse.

"I'm nothing like you think I am. This is just my job."

I run my hands across his shoulders and down his arms, my fingers searching for his. One step backwards gives me the space I need to compose my emotions, to explain to this sexy man that there's no room at the inn. Yet I don't say that. It's safer to skirt around such sensitive issues. Our fingers entwine.

"Come. Come with me." I release one of his hands and pick out a condom from a tub on the steel table, pull him to my dressing room, unable to look him in the eye, unable to let him view my soul windows. He mustn't see *me*.

We stop in front of the beanbag bed, and I toss the condom to land beside it and undo his shirt buttons — one...two...three — concertina its hem from his waist to his nipples. He raises his arms and removes his top while I — swift and adept — pop open his jean buttons and tug the fabric down his thighs. I latch my mouth onto his nipple, my teeth scraping his skin.

"Ah. Darkness, I — "

"Shhh." I lick his chest, his hairs rough on my chin, and the sensation reminds me of Ben's —

"I need you," he whispers, his voice hoarse with...

Lust. Yes, lust.

"You can have me. Any way you want in this room, as part of my job."

He steps out of his jeans, kicks off his shoes, and I, on tiptoes, attend to kissing his neck and manoeuvre him down onto the beanbag. Straddled over him, I rub my clit against his rigid cock, the fabric of his boxer shorts delicious friction. He teases my nipples through the rubber dress, his fingertips soft yet insistent, and gains eye contact for a brief moment before I wrench my gaze away and shift to enable the removal of his boxers.

I retrieve the condom, unwrap it, and, one-handed, roll it down his length. His breaths come in ragged gasps, and once again I straddle him, move the gusset of my thong aside, and plunge down on his cock. He groans and closes his eyes. He paws the air for a second then finds my waist, fingers kneading the base of my back, thumbs pressing into my lower abdomen, a perfect fit above my hip bones.

I grip his shoulders and begin a fast rhythm, wanting a quick, sweat-inducing fuck—no emotions, no attachments—to make him see this is all he'll ever get from me. In fact, that this is the last time I'll see him.

I can't do this anymore.

Bent on sating my own desires, using this man beneath me as a tool, I concentrate my all on chasing the goal, riding the crest, my gaze trained on his toned stomach muscles, imagining they're Ben's.

He whispers, "Shit, I love you."

"No," I pant, "you don't. You love...what I...represent. Not me. Not"—I ride him harder, faster, breaths shallow—"the real me."

He grunts as his cock throbs, and I clench around him, enticing him to come and come fast, join me at the pinnacle so I can get rid of him.

"Darkness, I—"

"Shut up. Just enjoy"—I inhale a deep breath through my nose...shit, I'm nearly there, nearly—"the ride."

He roves his hands from my waist to my stomach to my tits, a dance of temptation. I just need him for this, to satisfy my lust. After Friday, I'll never fuck Mark again.

My hole clenches around him once more, and the excitement, the drive to plunge him deeper inside me, builds. His tip bumps my cervix in sync with the tick of the second hand on the silver wall clock, and I cover his hands with mine—guide him, show him the pressure this fuck needs. No soft caresses, no loving ministrations, just harsh nipple tweaks, the strict kneading of flesh, and my wet cunt enveloping his exquisite prick. This is something, my gift to him, a fuck he'll remember for all time.

"Come on, Mark. Lose yourself with me. Come on."

"Uh. Ah, fuck, Darkness. You're so fucking...ah!" He bucks his pelvis, which jolts him deeper, his shaft slipping back and forth, delicious movements against that part inside of me that's due to spring forth a spurt of cum any time now.

I take my hands from his and dig my fingernails into the back of his neck, press my thumbs in the hollow above his clavicles. Movements faster now, faster still, I curl my toes, release so imminent I can *taste* it. I let my gaze move from his stomach to his face. He stares back at me, adoration obvious, and that's all I need to set me free. Control, I have it over him, and though it's wicked, though I'm using him...

I let loose a shout. My clit burns, my core swirls with rampant desire, and I yearn for a firmer touch on my nipples. I take his hands and direct them to my waist, place my own on my breasts and massage the flesh, twist my nipples. The rubber dress proving a hindrance, I ride him while removing it and throw it to the side. My breasts now free, we both move for them at the same time. He reaches them first, and, too far gone to care for his feelings, I snatch his fingers away and replace them with my own.

Hard nips and yanks are all I need to send me over the edge. He grasps my waist, rams me up and down, and just as my head lightens, as the wave builds to its highest point, his cock vein throbs and he yells a stuttered vocal of having reached his goal. I join him, releasing a satisfied "Ah!" each time my clit rubs his pubic hairs.

"Fuck. Fuck, that feels good." I pant, hands still loving my breasts, body jolting from the aftershocks.

"Darkness, I...I—"

"Shh!" Harsher than I'd intended. "This is it, Mark. No more."

* * * *

14ᵗʰ June — Morning

I've rushed back in here now that Mark has left to quickly scribble my thoughts down before my next client arrives. He tossed his payment onto the table by the door without looking at me, left without looking at me. What should I make of that? Maybe he didn't want me to see the hurt in his eyes. God, I sound like a pretentious bitch. It's more than likely he has shut me off and won't return, even with Gregg, now sex is off the table. I don't blame him.

His payment glared at me, and I swiped it up — it lays beside me on the beanbag bed now. I'll split it as usual with Madam. After all, I earned it.

Shit. Who am I kidding? I'd have loved a proper relationship with him at one time, but now? No way.

I sigh, admitting to myself that I've always had a soft spot for Mark. But it's too late.

I'm moving on, and will keep the secret that despite having Ben in my life, I've been indelibly Marked.

Chapter Fourteen

Jackpot

Last night's outfit was the right choice, so wearing something similar is my best bet. I go for a red sheath dress, fitted at the waist, which shows my bust off but only reveals the top of my cleavage. It'll leave a lot to Ben's imagination, and that can only add to the build-up of desire for Friday. If he's feeling anything like me, he'll be dying for a good fuck already.

I ponder on what he'd said, that he couldn't stop thinking about me while we are apart. It makes me all warm inside to know that. I'm not stupid, I know sex has a lot to do with it, but he must have found some other connection with me to admit he's falling in love so soon.

Imagine that! How strange life can be. He'd gone out to drown his sorrows and I'd gone out in search of cock. We'd both found something entirely different, and now our lives are on a different path, one where the potential for happiness and security is right within our grasps. I can't get over it.

Once again I take a taxi, relieved to see it isn't the pervert from the night before. It's an older guy, who smells of stale cigarettes and moth balls. He must have been a red-head in his day, because his beard still has strands of auburn in amongst the grey. Does he have a loving wife at home, hoping he stays safe in what could potentially be a dangerous job?

Will I grow old with Ben?

I berate myself for such a silly thought so early in the game.

But it would be nice, wouldn't it?

It would, and it's up to me to make sure I don't overpower him with my needs. The last thing I want is to get attached then scare him away just when I let my guard down completely.

The taxi draws up outside The Red Lion, and after paying the fare I take a minute to compose myself outside. I mustn't do anything tonight that involves sex. If I go to the toilet for privacy, I won't tell him that's what I'm doing. He'll most probably imagine anyway, but there's nothing I can do about that. I've set that chain of events in motion for every time I go to the ladies' and only have myself to blame. No, tonight I have to show him—and myself—that I can enjoy a night without being rude.

I'm kidding myself. There's no way I'm going to manage it.

Taking a deep breath, I go inside.

Ben isn't at the bar on his usual stool.

Panic gnaws at my gut, and I glance around casually, the action belying how I really feel inside.

Please let him just be late. I've pinned my hopes on this going right.

I sit at the bar and order a white wine, clutching the glass when it arrives, curling my fingers around the stem. My mouth and throat is dry, so I take a large gulp and hope the alcohol will steady my nerves. I look around the nearly deserted pub and wonder where everyone is tonight. Maybe there's something good on TV. That'd be a first.

The optics behind the bar take my attention, and I spend time counting them and the bottles below for something to do. Anything to take my mind off the possibility of being stood up. I think there's only about three drinks I've never tried there, and maybe, if this thing with Ben goes wrong, I'll buy those bottles and drink one a night so the alcohol takes me to that place where I don't have to think.

But what if something's happened? What if he's been hurt? What if he's been called out on a job and didn't have time to contact me? What if I didn't hear the message tone on my phone? A lot of *what ifs...*

I dig into my bag and look at my mobile.

No messages. No missed calls.

Shit.

Phone back in my bag, I realise the optic-counting game has lost its appeal. If he's much later, I'll be drinking a lot of fluid from those bottles, and if he doesn't turn up at all I'll go out and find a man to lose myself in just so I don't have to think about the pain. It's surprising how attached I've become—to Ben, to the idea of a relationship, a proper life outside the dungeon. It stuns me a little, just how much emotion I've invested without even realising it until now.

Ben is dangerous.

Ben could break my heart.

I stare at the bar top, circling a sticky beer stain with my fingertip, my heart thumping wildly and a sadness creeping up inside me that doesn't bode well.

"Hey you."

All the good emotions inside me stir at once. Happiness—no, make that me being ecstatic—relief, pleasure, oh, every damn wonderful thing you can imagine. I look into the mirror behind the bar and see him standing behind me, head tilted, him gazing down at me. He's wearing a different suit—dark grey this time—and he smells of a spicy aftershave I haven't encountered before.

I spin on the stool, one hand to my chest. "Oh! You're here!"

"And that surprises you because…?" He smiles.

"I thought you'd changed your mind," I blurt, cursing myself for being so honest then deciding what the hell, it's time to let go of old insecurities and just jump in so the whole of this experience envelops me, not matter how it turns out.

"Fucking hell, no." He sits on the stool beside me and takes my hand. "Are you hungry?"

"A little." I stare at his face, into those lovely eyes, and God, I want a hug so badly. One that tells me everything really is all right, that he really is here.

"Only a little?"

"Well, I'm hungrier than I was two minutes ago, put it that way."

"Good. Lift my hand."

Oh, God. Is he playing me at my own game? Has he —

"I was in the men's room. Needed some *privacy*."

Good Lord, he's walked out of my dreams and straight into my damn life. My clit throbs hard, and my nipples tighten painfully. I want him so much — *now, right now*—and the need for my own privacy grips me tight. I lift his hand to my mouth and run my tongue along the side. The taste of him floods my tongue, and I suck in a deep breath through my nose. I look up as I lick some more and see desire, pleasure and something I can't quite define in his eyes. That love he mentioned?

"God, kitten, I imagined you doing this the whole time I was jacking off."

My cunt floods. My breath hitches. The desire to fuck him takes a firmer hold, and I squirm on the stool. That doesn't help, only intensifies my need to come. The friction created from my labia rubbing together, nudging my clit, brings on the beginnings of an orgasm. I lick again, flattening my tongue this time, then suck two of his fingers deep into my mouth. It's like our surroundings have disappeared—only me and Ben exist. His cheeks flush, and he lets out a quiet, breathy moan.

"You...*you* are a guy's wet dream come true. Fuck, Klara."

I release his fingers, my cunt burning, my heart rate speeding. "We need to get out of here. Into the fresh air." I let his hand fall and grab my wine, swallowing it quickly. I'd visit the ladies' but don't think I'll make it in time. "Hurry up!" I dash out of the pub and wait for him, an orgasm building without any stimulation except my raging thoughts.

I'm going to have to break my own rule.

He walks out into the night, and I grab his hand.

"Down here!" I lead him along an alley beside the pub. The ground is uneven, and I stumble a little in my heels.

"What the hell?"

"You need to do something about this." I point to my groin even though I doubt he can see me in the darkness. "The ladies' isn't going to cut it."

"But you said—"

"I know what I said, but what do you expect when you do something like that?" I walk him a little further.

"So it's all right for you to do it to me!"

"Yes! You don't have the same problem as I have, do you?"

"No, but hanging around with you might change that pretty damn quickly."

I stop at the end of the alley and press my back to the wall of The Red Lion. "Well, you'd better lick my cunt pretty damn quickly before I... Shit, just hurry up!"

I pull up my dress and splay my legs. Cool air caresses my heated pussy, but I want more warmth there—his tongue delving, licking, his breaths making my slit even hotter.

"Jesus fucking Christ!" Ben hunkers down in front of me. "You smell so damn strong."

"Stop the talking and just... Oh!"

He buries his mouth in my folds, tongue sliding up and down then circling my clit. He manages two rotations before my close-as-hell orgasm gets even closer.

"Oh, my God, Ben. That's it. Faster! Lick faster. Harder."

He moans against me, the sound sending echoic pulses into my hard and needy bud. I slap my hands onto the wall—the brick rough on my palms, fingertips and bare arse. His tongue is just as rough, a beautiful abrasion on my sensitive nerves, and as he licks and circles, I can't hold off any longer. My orgasm explodes with me looking down and seeing his shadowy head bobbing. He grips my outer thighs, laving frantically, and I pant and groan, hips bucking. My legs weaken, and I shriek as another wave of pleasure sears my cunt.

"Oh, fuck, Ben. That's so good. You're so good."

A third wave flows, more violent than the last, and I lose the ability to breathe for a second or two. My head lightens, tiny white spots dance in the air, and I clamp my hands onto his head to stop myself falling sideways. He licks on, slowing as though he knows I've hit the peak and I'm coming down. While I concentrate on breathing properly and experiencing the final, beautiful tendrils of fading bliss, he stops completely and stands. Kisses me, transferring my juices to my mouth. I taste tart, a sharp blend of musk and salt. I kiss him hard and fast, crossing my arms behind his neck and sliding my hands through the back of his hair. The gel makes it feel prickly, and I look forward to the time when he hasn't got any products in it.

With the need to suck in a huge breath, I break the kiss and rest my head against the wall. I pant, looking at his silhouette while he pulls down my dress and smoothes it into place.

"That was… God, I can't even describe what that was," I say.

"Hot as fuck. It's a good job I visited the men's room, because otherwise you wouldn't have even managed to return the favour. I'd have come in my pants."

"Do you want me to…?"

"No. I'm being good. I can wait until Friday. You can't."

My heart melts just a little bit at his understanding of my condition. How the hell did I get so lucky?

I cup his face and draw him close. "I wanted to be so good. I didn't intend for this to happen. Tonight was supposed to be us talking, finding things out about each other."

"We still can. The table isn't booked until eight." He brushes a brief kiss on my lips. "Are you all right to go now?"

I rest my forehead on his chest. "Yes."

"Come on then."

He clasps my hand, holding it tight, and leads the way out of the alley. I think about his talented tongue and can only imagine what else he has to offer in the bedroom. With his consideration for my feelings, I *don't* have to imagine how he'll be with regard to my emotions. He's caring and sensitive, that much is clear.

It isn't only him who's hit the jackpot, Klara.

As we emerge from the alley, the streetlights bringing his face into perfect view, I look at him and have the sudden need to cry. He frowns and takes me in his arms, an immediate action that tells me he's in tune with me, can sense what I'm feeling.

"It's okay," he says, pressing me to his chest and stroking my hair. "Everything will be okay. I'll take care of you, provide everything you need. Just trust me. Meeting you…shit, it's been a revelation, I'll give you that much, but it's so much more than anything I thought I'd ever get. We've only known each other a couple of days but it feels like weeks. D'you have that feeling?"

I think about it and nod, tears on the verge of spilling. "I never thought…never thought this love thing would happen to me. That I'd find a man like you. It's all happening so fast it's crazy."

"Good crazy, though, right?"

I nod again. "Fucking good crazy."

"So," he says, pulling back. "Restaurant?"

"Sounds good, but to be honest I'd rather eat somewhere more comfortable."

"Will my place do you? It isn't much, just a small flat, but I like it."

"Yes, that's fine."

"I'll just ring the restaurant and cancel our table. Want to get a takeaway?"

"Anything will do. A sandwich is fine. You don't have to go to any trouble."

"Hmmm. Says the woman who insisted on being wined and dined."

"Aww, come on now. I didn't expect things to go the way they have."

He chuckles and strokes my cheek with the backs of his fingers. "You like Indian food?"

"Love it."

"Let's go then." He pulls out his phone, and as we walk towards the Indian takeaway, calls to cancel our table.

God, I love this man.

* * * *

We sit side by side on Ben's puffy red sofa, him with a korma and me with the spicier jalfrezi. His flat is cosy, lived in...like a home should be. His plumber's tool bag sits beside one of the armchairs opposite, the corner of it peeking out from beneath a lazily slung black jacket. The cartons from our meal are strewn haphazardly on a low pine coffee table, glasses of cola sitting on top of mismatched coasters. I scrunch my toes into the deep pile of his beige carpet and pop a mouthful of curry into my mouth. It's delicious—almost as delicious as Ben—and I'm comfortable for the first time in ages.

"This is nice, isn't it? Sitting here like this," he says.

"It is. The food's good, too."

He nods and takes another bite, swallowing before he asks, "So, your job. You like it?"

I'd wondered if this would be a bone of contention between us. Not many men could put up with their other half servicing male clients.

"It serves a purpose...it's really that simple. I couldn't think what I could do to help me out, you know? And that's the job I came up with. I learned from Madam what to do—I'd never been involved in BDSM before—and although I enjoy the actual job, the fucking is just...well, it's just something I need to do. I don't feel anything for them. They use me as much as I use them. Just that I get paid for it."

There was no point in sugar-coating it.

"Right, so, you said before that after Friday, if we got on well and whatever, you wouldn't fuck your clients anymore."

"And I meant it. If I don't need to—"

"You won't. Do you enjoy the job enough to continue it if you don't need to be there?"

I shrug. "I think so, but at the same time it's just a job, something I do. I wouldn't have a clue what else to try if I left."

"It's just that... My thoughts on it are typical. If we...when we become a proper item, I can't for the life of me imagine being comfortable with what you're doing."

I open my mouth to speak, but he holds up his hand, fork pointed skywards.

"Hear me out, yeah?" He takes a deep breath. "But at the same time, this is your job—something you did when we met—and I don't have the right to tell you to change careers. I went out with you knowing what you do, so for me to say I'd hate it if you continued doesn't feel right."

"But you'd hate it anyway, right?"

"I'd hate the thought of other men touching you, yes. When you're mine. D'you understand what I mean? I won't be telling you what to do, but thought I'd better let you know how it sits with me. But also, if you choose to stay at your job, I don't want it to ever come between us. I'll just have to learn to deal with it. Providing you're not fucking them. Now that *would* bother me."

"I understand and wouldn't expect anything else. I told you, once we're an item…hell, every other man fucking me just isn't an option. Madam will understand. She'll be surprised as hell, but she won't expect me to service clients in that way."

He sighs, with relief I'll bet. "But what I'm trying to say is, do you enjoy what you do with them? I mean, what *do* you do?"

"Spanking, chaining them up, hitting them—lots of men like face slaps—gagging them. Lots of things."

"And you like it?"

"Yes, I do."

"So, if you had the chance to do those things outside of work, would you take it?"

Is he saying…? "You mean, if I could do those things with you, would that be enough?"

"Yes." He blushes and looks down at his plate. "I've never done anything like that before. You'd have to teach me. Would you want to do that?"

"Fuck, yes!"

He looks across at me. "But I might not be any good."

"Oh, you'll be good."

He smiles sheepishly. "I don't know, but we could try, couldn't we?"

"Damn right we can."

We continue eating, my mind full of how quickly things have changed. Come Friday, I won't have to work in the dungeons if I don't want to. And do I? No, not really. If I can get what I need at home, what's the point of being a working Domme? Besides, I have to admit the thought of Ben struggling to cope with knowing what I could be doing while he's fixing a broken boiler or fitting someone's new shower…

No. I can't do that to him.

I swallow the last piece of chicken and lay my fork down. Ben does the same, and I take his plate and put them both on the coffee table. I snuggle up beside him, one leg draped over both of his, and feel complete as his arm goes around me and he hugs me closer.

"I can't wait until Friday," I say.

"Me neither."

"Not just for…you know."

"No, I know. Friday is the beginning of our new life together. *That's* what I can't wait for, kitten."

Chapter Fifteen

Shadows
15th June — Morning

I took a bath again last night and promised myself to have no more thoughts of things going wrong. Threads of Ben, his very fabric, have now weaved into the material of my heart.

This morning, I stand on the beach that represents my life, toes warmed by the sun-kissed sand. A new dawn brings a fresh horizon — clear, unsullied by fog or mist, the sky stark bright, my watery emotions calm. As of this moment, everything is right with my world.

```
Name: Roger Liston
Preference: Anything goes.
Notes: He suffers from the male version of my
affliction—satyriasis. I only entertain him as an
extra in Shadow's dungeon.
```

Naked, knees up, legs splayed, I lie on the red leather bed and ponder how long it will take for Shadow to beckon me into her dungeon. I usually stand in the hallway outside her door ten minutes after Mr Liston arrives and await her call. His preference says anything goes, but every time I've joined them, he's firmly planted inside Miss Suzy, gaze flicking from Shadow to me, me to Shadow. His eyes bulge as though he's unable to quite believe two women—three if you count his reasoning that Miss Suzy is real—occupy his space, all of us there for him alone.

How special he must feel. Mind you, I heard that for him a fuck is a fuck—just something he does to release the incessant itch that urges blood into his cock at inopportune times of the day. At least I can hide my arousal. It must be harder for a man, pun intended. Both of us need a good seeing-to too many times a day, and having sex with someone who isn't desirable on the eye doesn't enter the equation when it's just a case of quenching my thirst for release. For me, tension builds to such high proportions that I'd shag anyone. Until Ben came along.

I now have the chance at a relationship where I stay true to one person. Shadow has found her ideal, wrapped up in the package that is Beautiful Luke. He's a special man who knows how to treat a woman. I wish…I wish I wasn't a nymphomaniac.

Shadow once told me, "Luke always hesitates before he comes into my room. I think he debates whether or not he should come in. Or whether he should walk away, leave the dungeons, and never come back."

I can't tell her why he used to be so reticent to enter her room, knowing mine is right next door. He used to visit me before Shadow worked at the dungeons. Perhaps he felt guilty, thought I'd think he'd abandoned me when the black-haired beauty came along. I can't tell her why he likes the singer, Pink, either. Why he asks for her songs to be played while she canes his feet and makes him come.

"You look like her," he said to me once, his legs on show in shorts, his bare chest chiselled and tanned. He shifted on the bed to turn and look at me. "Well, you would if you had the same hairstyle."

Pink, on the stereo at the time, sang her heart out, her midriff on show.

"Imagine her, Darkness," he'd said. "Think how sexy she is. Just like you."

He'd inclined his head, called me over, and took me in his arms. Luke had made love to me then—a vast difference from what I've experience with other clients. Yes, he treated me so well, and I…I threw it all away. Shadow knows I've fucked him. I can only hope she realises there's nothing left between me and her man. Was never anything there in the first place—for me, anyway. He was a means to an end.

I switch my thoughts to Ben, let my fingers stray to my slit and stroke the folds, tease myself with the slightest brush. My other hand finds my breasts, nails raking one nipple with harsh jerks that shoot pleasure from the hard nub down to my clit. I clench my hole in a lazy rhythm, and my clit engorges, sensitive as my thumb glides over it. I could just give in to desire and come now, but I won't. Mr Liston has already arrived, and time isn't on my side.

Off the bed now, I make my way to stand outside Shadow's dungeon. My ear against the door, the sounds from within indicate how long I'll have to loiter out here. Luckily only our dungeons occupy this floor.

"Oh, you're so good to me, sharing me with your friend, Miss Suzy." Mr Liston sounds overly excited again.

I know the feeling.

"Bring her to me. Let me taste her," he croons. "Miss Suzy, you sexy bitch. I'm going to make you come so hard, my little beauty, that you'll never want for another man again."

"Don't lick her," Shadow says. "She wants you inside her. She told me how hot it makes her when your cock fills her soft, sexy cunt."

I fondle my sex, my tits, and lick my lips, eyes closed.

I wish Ben was here.

"Ah! Oh, she feels so good. So...tight." Mr Liston pants, and the squeak of the leather bed filters through the door, the sound intent on teasing me mercilessly. Images flicker through my mind of Mr Liston firmly inserted inside Miss Suzy, his arse clenching, his toes splayed. I pinch my nipples — hard — and release a low moan.

Shit, I'm going to come soon, imaging Ben is writhing on that bed. I bite my lower lip and concentrate on the pain, take my hands away from myself and ball them into fists at my sides.

"Would you like another treat?" Shadow asks. "Another friend of mine would like to join us. Would you enjoy that?"

"Oh, oh," Liston grinds out, and the bed squeaks again, each creak of cowhide merging into the next. "Yes. Fuck, yes. I want to lick her, make her come."

"Darkness!" Shadow calls.

I'm in the room, my sights on Shadow. She stands to the right side of the bed, eyes trained on the doorway, on me. Her gaze roves from my face to my pussy, and she widens her eyes.

"Why, Darkness! How lovely of you to join us. I do believe, by the wetness of your slit, that you've started before us."

I smile, wink, and look at Mr Liston, who pumps away at Miss Suzy while craning his head to catch a glimpse of me. I walk towards Shadow — my heart rate accelerated — and trail my fingertips from Liston's heels, up his hairy calf, his thick thigh, to his waist. His body jerks faster, spasms, and he sets free an agonised groan.

"Oh, fuck. Fuck, hurry! Miss Suzy is so tight, and you, your wet hole...let me touch it. Let me lick it, tongue it." His eyes beseech me, his floppy hair dancing with his gyrations. Sweat forms on his brow. A bead meanders down his temple and veers into his hairline.

I so don't want to be here anymore, but despite that, I can't deny I'm turned on.

I raise an eyebrow at Shadow, and she gives the slightest of nods, so I trace a line from Liston's waist up his back and sashay to stand at the head end of the bed. My sex begs to be licked, and Mr Liston's mouth answers the plea, covers my slit, his cock thrusting in and out of Miss Suzy. Staccato breaths exit Shadow's mouth, and Mr Liston sucks and pumps, gaining speed and rhythm.

"Darkness, go and stand behind Shadow. Quickly," Mr Liston says.

I look at Shadow. Our gazes lock. She doesn't usually allow anything to happen between us. Is today going to be different?

She smiles, shakes her head.

Liston's lips and tongue take care of the fire in my cunt. Shadow walks to stand behind me. She brings her warm hands up my sides and places them on my stomach. And that's all she'll do. It's an illusion for Liston to believe he's in a true foursome.

I encircle my nipples with languid motions then flick-scratch-flick. The sensation I adore lures my nipples to straighter attention, wicked sexual spell surrounding me. I imagine the scent of my arousal as a tangible thing, a coil of smoke as it spirals up and greets my nose.

I reach forward and clutch Liston's hair with one hand. He ups the pace—his tongue wreaks riotous havoc on my clit, the circular motions wonderful. His arse clenches with each thrust into Miss Suzy, the sight unleashing the boiling desire to come hard.

"Uh, uh, ah...beautiful pussy, tastes so good," Liston mumbles against me.

"Don't. Stop," I say. "Suck me. Tongue me."

"Fuck, you're sexy!" Liston shouts then dives into my folds again, the movements of his tongue harder, more fervent.

I grip his hair tighter and continue the flick-scratch-flick on my nipple. I look down at my tits, the sight of my red painted nails an erotic image along with Mr Liston's face buried in my folds.

"Ah, shit. I can't...can't hold off any longer." I bite my bottom lip.

Fever seems to touch so many places—my breasts, my hole, my clit, everywhere—and Shadow moves away, one step back. It doesn't matter where she stands now. Mr Liston is too far gone to notice. I jerk against Liston's lapping tongue and scratch my nipple harder.

"Oooh. Fuck, yesss!" I hiss, hair draped over my shoulder. "I'm coming!"

My hole spasms around Liston's tongue. He pumps into Miss Suzy, frantic, and his breathy "Uh! Oh, baby, yes!" further increases my excitement. I'm up, climbing the peak, the top right there...

I crash over it, my pelvis shuddering with contractions, pushed out for Liston to finish me off.

He shouts out a moan against my pussy, then, "Beautiful Darkness!"

We grow still, our breathing heavy. Mr Liston drops his temple to the bed and grips Miss Suzy's handgrip tighter, his knuckles white, his chin damp with my juices. He scrunches his eyes closed, and one more thrust sees him spent, a juddering mess. With Liston's mouth gone, cold air chills my wet cunt.

"Well," I say, "that was—"

"Quite delightful, ladies!" Mr Liston finishes and rolls off Miss Suzy, a satisfied grin on his face.

"Yes." Shadow stares at me, a frown firmly in place. "Quite delightful."

I cock my head and instantly know why her voice holds no conviction.

She's as sick of this job as I am.

* * * *

15th June — Afternoon

The previously calm setting of my world has changed once more. The horizon has gained a rolling mist, obscuring my future — I can't see where I'm headed. The sand between my toes is cold now, for the sun has hidden behind a bank of grey clouds. It brings thoughts to mind of needing shoes on my feet to protect them from a possibly rocky path that emerges along the beach a little way. Guilt has arrived. Although I gained pleasure from Liston, I hate myself for letting him bring me off. I feel I should already be true to Ben. It feels wrong to allow other men to touch me, knowing Ben might be torturing himself with images he'd rather not see. We're not a proper item yet, but still, we will be.

Friday can't come soon enough.

Being a Domme was a stop gap, somewhere to pass the time until I won the real prize. I'm no better than Shadow, then, staying here when there is absolutely no need. What is it about this place that holds us? Or is it nothing to do with the dungeons and the clients who visit? Perhaps both of us are afraid of it going wrong so strongly that our jobs provide security.

Maybe we both need to trust more, to take a leap of faith and hope for the best.

The shadows of my past shroud me, hiding the truth.

I'm frightened.

So I think of Ben.

The sun peeks over the clouds and illuminates my world again. A gusty southwester blows away the mist, and land is discernible, far, far away. Ben stands on an island in the distance, but I must travel over the sea to reach him.

I imagine myself jumping into the water with a choice.

Sink or swim.

Chapter Sixteen

Knocked for Six

I can't wait to see Ben again. The guilt from Liston and the other men who followed him has eaten at me all day. I shouldn't have allowed them to have sex with me, but like Madam said this morning, they'd arrived thinking they would get what they were paying over the odds for. The other Dommes who gave out couldn't fit the extras onto their schedules until Madam rearranges them next week or hires someone new. I'll fulfil my obligations until Friday and that's it. I'll just have to push the guilt aside. The problem is, once my libido is up and running — when isn't it? — I give myself over to it completely.

I have to teach myself not to. Who knows, maybe once Ben and I are official, my body will match my mindset. If I know I'm going to have sex with him at least once a day, I should be able to manage with private moments all other times.

Shouldn't I?

If I think I can't, I need to be honest with Ben. It isn't fair on him if I go behind his back. I see he's taking a huge step being with me and I'm grateful he thinks enough of me to do that. Putting himself at risk. All it would take is one slip on my part and the happiness and security I crave with him will be gone.

Trust. I have to earn it and keep it.

Tonight I'm wearing casual clothes, having agreed with Ben via text this morning that we'll hang out at my apartment. Shadow is at the theatre with Luke, then staying over at his place, so there will be no interruptions.

I'm nervous again. Ben coming over means sharing my space. What if he doesn't like it here? It isn't the same as sharing it with Shadow. She spends most of her time in her room now, talking on the phone with Luke if he's working late. Earlier, when she was getting ready, I passed her door and heard her side of a conversation. I guessed it was Luke from what she'd said. Shadow plans to move out but doesn't know how to tell me. Of course, she has no idea yet about Ben and that her moving out wouldn't even have been a problem had Ben not been around. I want Shadow to have the life she's always dreamed of—she's my best friend, for God's sake—so why would her moving on upset me?

I must find the time to speak with her, let her know what's going on so she isn't worrying about breaking the news to me.

I smooth my hands down my comfortable black jeans and once again straighten the hem of my white vest top so it rests nicely on my hips. I've coiled my hair into an up-do tonight, a messy mop with tendrils hanging down. Leaving my feet bare—pointless putting heels on, and I most certainly do not want to greet him wearing my furry white slipper boots—I pace in front of the large living room window overlooking the car park.

Ben is due in about five minutes, but I don't want to miss his arrival, the chance to see him before he sees me. If he looks smart and I feel underdressed, I can quickly change before he knocks on the apartment door. I don't know why I feel so self-conscious, why him seeing me in casuals is a problem. I suppose it's because he's only ever seen me dressed up. Maybe, subconsciously, I didn't make much of an effort on purpose. If he likes me in what I'm wearing, he'll like me in anything. It'll prove he likes me for me.

My mind is all over the place, me thinking one thing then contradicting it in the next breath. Is this what love is like? What it does to you?

I don't know. I've never been in love before, not really.

Am I in love?

The swathe of headlamps cuts through the darkness outside, and I jump a little. The driver parks up, the headlights douse, and a figure emerges from the vehicle. It's Ben, I know it, would recognise that silhouette anywhere after our time in the alley. My stomach bunches and I swallow a fit of nerves. My hands shaking doesn't help matters, so I knit my fingers and squeeze.

He strides towards the apartment block, coming into the light of the streetlamps positioned in a row of four directly outside the main doors. He looks around, and I just about make out by his expression he wasn't expecting me to live somewhere like this. He'll be realising about now just how much money I can earn—or wondering if I'm some rich, wild child brat who lives off a trust fund.

No, I'm not a rich brat. I earned every penny, have saved enough to buy this apartment outright.

I've been in this business far too long.

I sigh and wait for the doorbell. It comes just as I wonder whether he's gone to the wrong apartment. The jarring buzz frazzles my nerves some more. Why the hell do I feel like this? It's not as if I haven't met him before.

It's him seeing me in my own environment, that's what it is. Seeing how I live, my tastes, whether I do enough housework or not. So I'm wondering if he'll be checking out my place to see if I'm good housewife material, is that it? Am I hoping for that much?

Yes, I am.

I scurry to the door, taking a deep breath at the same time as tidying my clothes yet again. I worry whether my face has flushed a little too red—it feels like it's burning—and whether my hairstyle has drooped. I worry whether I showered well enough to get the scent of those damn men off me—men I wished I'd never fucked now. I worry about every little thing.

Open the damn door!

I pull it open and feast my eyes on him. He's wearing jeans too, and a tight-fitting black T-shirt that shows off his brawny chest. Holy hell, he's going to be the death of me.

"Wow," I breathe. "Don't you just look good enough to eat?"

I didn't mean that sexually, really I didn't. It just popped out.

"Same goes for you. Can I be blunt?" he asks, stepping inside.

"Of course." I close the door and turn to face him.

"Your tits look damn fine in that top."

His words hit me right in my cunt.

"Shit, Ben! I told myself I'd be good tonight, and there you go, saying something like that!"

"Sorry. Can't help it." He holds up a takeaway bag. "Thought Chinese would be good." He raises another bag. "And white wine. I noticed you always drink it."

"Are you changing the subject by any chance?"

Shit, my clit aches.

"Isn't it wise to?"

"I suppose it is."

Reluctantly, I turn away and lead him into the living room.

"Make yourself at home while I go and get some plates."

I almost run into the kitchen, slamming myself against the wall and pressing the heel of my hand to my cunt. I close my eyes, taking deep breaths. My jeans abrade my clit, and I rub, allowing a small but satisfying orgasm to drift over me. It isn't nearly enough, but it takes the edge off. My breathing laboured, I open my eyes with the intention of grabbing the plates and some cutlery.

Ben is standing in the doorway. "Was that as good for you as it was for me?"

My cheeks blaze hotter than they were when I opened the front door. "Oh, crap. You weren't supposed to—"

"Thought I'd come and give you a hand with the plates. I didn't expect to see you like that, but fucking hell, I'm glad I did." He walks over to me, pinning me to the wall with his body, erection hard on my belly. He flattens his hands on the wall either side of my head. "Do you know how damn sexy you are? How knowing that at any time I could walk in on you masturbating? That any time we're apart I can imagine you touching yourself, almost guaranteeing that's what you're doing. D'you even realise how bloody horny that is?"

I look up at him, my heart pounding. "I suppose. But I'd have thought it would make you feel, I don't know, not enough for me."

"I'll never be enough, kitten—we both know that. I've been thinking about it, have accepted it. I care about you so much already that if you really can't manage without other men…well, I'll make myself get over it. So long as it's me you come home to, me you love, that's what matters."

Oh my God. That is one special gift he's offering me.

"No. It's you and you alone from Friday. I mean it, Ben. Thank you, thank you so much for understanding, but I can't keep hiding from my problem and dealing with it the way I have been. It's mind over body. I just need to learn to control it." It's time to open up some more. "D'you know, today, when I…when I was working, it didn't feel right. Like I was betraying you. I knew I had the green light to do it, knew it was just to scratch an itch, but God, you were on my mind."

"Then that's not so bad, is it? If you're fucking a client and thinking of me, that doesn't count, right?"

"You *want* me to fuck other men?"

"No, God no, but I'm trying to figure out ways of being supportive and at the same time coping with any decision you make. If being with you means sharing you, then I'll take it. I don't want to lose you now I've found you."

I sag into him, putting my arms around his back and clutching his T-shirt into my fists. I want to cry. How the hell did I get so lucky? I've asked myself this before, but this time…God, how many men out there would shove their feelings aside like that in order to be with a woman?

"I can't do it," I mumble into his chest. "Don't want to do it anymore. I'm only doing it now because I feel I have to. Letting Madam down when she's been so good to me. It was kind of mechanical today, me just going through the motions. There wasn't any feeling involved before, I just did it. But since I've met you… I don't know, the feelings have come, where I want you to be the one fucking me, you to be touching me. It's so difficult. I have the urges, can't get rid of them, and I wish to God I could."

"Hey!" He strokes the back of my head then slips a finger beneath my chin and raises my face so I'm looking at him. "We'll get through this. I'll make you better, help you to cope, all right?"

I nod, and then the tears finally spill. He wipes them away with his thumbs, lowering his head to press a soft kiss on my mouth. For once I don't want the hot-as-hell touch of a tongue against mine, the heady rush of a searing kiss. That brief touch is enough.

"You've knocked me for six, Ben," I whisper.

"Good." He smiles and kisses the tip of my nose. "So, we'll eat, right? Continue our date?"

I nod and let his T-shirt go. "Sorry, I'll have made your top all crinkled."

"Like I give a shit about that."

His gentle smile makes my tummy roll over.

I think I love him.

* * * *

Once again, dinner was delicious. Ben had bought a selection of dishes, and there's enough left over for a snack after work tomorrow if the fancy takes me. As I nestle beside him on the sofa, my legs curled beneath me, one arm behind his back and the other draped over his stomach, I face the bold truth.

I'm dreading work tomorrow.

I breathe deeply to take my fill of his scent. I love his aftershave and make a mental note to look in his bathroom or bedroom next time I'm there to find out what it is. I'll buy some to keep at home, and when we're apart and I'm missing him, I can open the bottle.

I sound a weird bunny boiler, but I don't care.

"I don't want to go to work tomorrow, Ben."

"Aww, kitten. You can do this. *We* can do this. Just one more day. Have you thought what else you'd like to do instead?"

He fiddles with my hair, and I'm surprised it doesn't make me want to jump his bones. A first for me. Maybe this mind over body thing will work after all. Or maybe it's because I'm with him, knowing I could fuck him if I wanted. I'll soon see tomorrow when he isn't there.

"No. I have no idea."

"Give it time. Maybe have a few weeks off to get used to not being there. Take some days for yourself."

"My mind being idle isn't a good idea. It might wander. I don't want that. It could lead to me showing up while you're working or spending all my time in bed with my hand between my legs." I have to make a joke of it. If I don't, if I think of what's going on with me as some kind of disease, then it'll beat me.

I can master this thing if Ben's by my side.

His laugh, rich and much loved, fills the room. "A hand between your legs doesn't sound like such a bad idea at all. Especially if it's mine."

Now that *does* make me want to jump his bones.

"Tomorrow night's too far away, isn't it." I trace a line up his chest with my fingertip, clit throbbing.

"But when we get there, look at what's ahead. No more insecurity. Us two together. Can't be bad. This time last week, shit, you can imagine the state I was in. And you, struggling to work out what the hell to do when things got too much. It's all good, Klara. Everything's going to work out, you'll see."

In his arms like this, his closeness taking everything bad away, I can agree with him. Everything *is* going to be all right.

"Did you always want to be a plumber?" I ask in a bid to stave off the strong stirrings of desire.

"No more than you always wanting to be a Domme. It was just something I drifted into. A mate needed a hand, I was out of a job and went along, found it easy and there you go."

"What *did* you want to do?" *I want to know everything about you, every single thing.*

"Be a banker, believe it or not. Or work in the Stock Exchange. I've got the brains for it, just that things didn't work out that way. I left university, all buoyed up that I'd walk into a great job and earn shitloads of money, but the market wasn't too good for job prospects and I ended up working in a bloody bar. I lost that job when the brewery went tits up. Then the plumbing job came along, I did a course for it, and that's what I've been doing ever since."

"Don't you ever think about trying for banking again, seeing if you can break into it?" *You smell lovely.*

"Sometimes, but hey, plumbers pull in quite a wage. My place might not reflect that, doubt my car does either, but I'm not doing too badly." He pauses to kiss the top of my head. "Come on, think. There must be something you've always wanted to do."

I sigh. "The usual girly thing. Hairdresser, beautician. Honestly, there's nothing springing to mind here."

"What about being a plumber's mate?"

I sit up and stare at him, my mouth hanging open. "Are you serious? Me, a plumber's mate?"

"Why not? Women are doing so-called men's jobs all the time."

"I know, but come on! You're joking, aren't you?"

"Nope. It'd mean you spend all day with me. And when you need privacy...well, you wouldn't have to have privacy. We could jump in the back of the van."

Oh my God. It's an insane prospect, but hell, it's growing on me by the second.

Take a leap of faith...

"Fuck it. All right. I'll do it."

He laughs again and takes my face in his hands. "I knew the van thing would sway you."

I swat his chest. "You bastard!"

"Yeah, but you love me, right?" He looks at me hopefully.

"D'you know, I think I do."

Chapter Seventeen

Knots
16th June — Morning

It's official. I'm going to leave this job and start elsewhere. It's the only way I can put the past behind me. The memories will still linger for a while, I'm sure, but I'm hoping they'll eventually fade.

I blamed my affliction, when in reality I could have sought medical help. I must not have wanted to. Maybe admitting it to a doctor was too embarrassing. Still, there comes a time when we must re-evaluate our lives and take stock of what was, is, and can be. I prefer to embrace my life with Ben rather than face the truths that stare me in the face now.

That I was weak and took the easy route. Sated my desires, telling myself it was my only choice.

Lies, all lies.

```
Name: Gerry Sanders
Preference: Riding crop, blindfold, silk scarves.
Notes: Gerry is a nice man, bent on pleasing me
as well as himself. I imagine he would make a
good husband, though he assures me his wife hates
him, doesn't understand him. Shame he doesn't
realise I've heard it all before one hundred
times over.
```

This is the last day that I'll stand before this wardrobe, the last day I'll select these outfits, screw my clients, and take their hard-earned cash for doing me a favour. Their money pays my rent, buys food, clothing, and nice things for my apartment. Their presence did so much more — more than any pill could. Or so I tell myself. I think, more than just having nymphomania, I became addicted to sex. Like a drug, it calms me, gives a heady rush, and makes me whole, if only for the hour or so between urges.

Perhaps with the steady flow of sex from Ben in my future will change all that. Maybe I can learn to control myself more. Maybe when someone loves you, truly loves you, the need for sex isn't so strong. Perhaps knowing I can have sex any time I want with Ben will be enough to make the constant need for it ease off a bit. Despite emotions getting in the way with clients lately, I want to do my job to the best of my ability right until the end. They come to me wanting a good fuck, and if I give them anything less it'll be like I'm robbing them of not only money but their expectations too. And it's funny, but although I'm heading out of here later free from *having* to do what these walls have witnessed day in, day out, I may well miss these men. Not them touching me — no, never that — but them as people. For too long I've seen their faces, seen their emotions displayed plainly, said hello and waved goodbye, them a constant in my life and me in theirs. We helped one another out and I owe it to them not to disappoint during our last meetings.

So, today I'm going out with a bang. I decide to give Mr Sanders a treat and greet him naked. I'm going to try and switch off my emotions, be like I was before I met Ben. Just a Domme who's here to do her job and get these men off...get myself off.

He knocks on the door, his tentative rap belying his burly body and demeanour.

"Enter!"

The door swings open, and the gloomy landing renders his body a silhouette in the doorway. He reminds me of a giant. His curly black hair almost touches the lintel. Once he takes a step inside, the glow of the single bulb in my dungeon cajoles his strong features out of the darkness. A tropical tan browns his skin—a recent holiday to Mauritius, if my memory serves me correctly—and his open-necked, short-sleeved shirt allows me a good look at his thick arms and wide neck. I wonder if the gym alone has enhanced his physique or whether he's naturally large and buff.

A shiver of anticipation zips through me at memories of how his stout cock feels inside me. How his girth stretches my hole to the point of pain—pain I've enjoyed in the past because it ultimately gives way to pleasure.

Stop it. Think of this as just a job and not something you're doing for pleasure.

My nipples betray my emotions, and Mr Sanders' gaze roams from them to my slit.

"Morning, Mistress Darkness. What a pleasure to see you like...this."

His gruff voice makes my hole spasm, and warmth spreads from my core up into the pit of my stomach. A lazy smile curves his lips. He closes the door behind him, then places his payment on the table beside it.

"Good morning, Gerry." I stare at him, take in every line of his face. I'm fond of Mr Sanders, fond of this place. It helped me through my darkest times. In one way, leaving here will be a wrench. I'm putting my trust in Ben. My whole life in his hands.

The backs of my eyes sting, and images of all those who have sated my desires flicker through my mind. I have given a part of myself over to them, but have taken so much more. Ground my clit against various body parts, rubbed my nipples against backs, arms, chests. Yet I look back on it and feel that despite it being right at the time, it's all kinds of wrong now.

It's just a job. Just a job.

"Get undressed. Hurry." I lick my lips, slide a finger between them, and bite down. I need the pain to take my mind off what I'm about to do. Yes, I've told myself today's fucks are for old time's sake—my duty, something I need to do in order to walk away knowing I gave them a good service—but... Shit, I'm wondering whether I can do that now. That gnawing sense of betrayal has emerged, spiralling inside me, spreading its tendrils in my gut, their ends stretching up, down and out to encompass every bit of me. I feel slightly sick and wish the end of the day was now so I don't have to go through the next few hours.

What's Ben doing? Is he thinking of me, tying himself up in knots knowing what I'm about to do? Or has he shut it out of his head, deciding instead to concentrate on the job at hand rather than torment himself? Am I being fair to him, doing this today? Should I tell all the clients there's been a change of plan and there's no sex on the menu today—sorry about that but I've met this wonderful fella and I don't need your cocks, your hands, your tongues anymore?

Guilt. A damaging thing.

He raises his eyebrows and widens his smile. He moves towards me and trails his finger between my breasts, down to my navel, lower still, halting at the juncture of my thighs. I inhale a sharp breath and marvel at the size of his pupils, dilated with the promise of what is to come.

Just do it. Get it over with.

"Do you want to stay in here or go into my dressing room?" I ask.

Mr Sanders looks at the ceiling, contemplates for a second, and says, his voice husky, "Mistress Darkness, in the dungeon, with the whip."

His allusion to the board game Cluedo incites a smile to my lips.

"And which character are you today?" I roll my tongue around my fingertip, wondering how the hell I've coped with this scenario in the past. The prize of sex must have made me blind to how ridiculous it all is.

"Mr Sexy, on the bed, with the silk scarves." He strokes my Brazilian, his gaze penetrative. He seems to read my soul, know something is wrong. He frowns. "Are you all right?"

"Of course! As I said, hurry and get undressed."

He inclines his head, shrugs, and brushes past me and into the changing room. The curtain swooshes across the doorway, and his clothing rustles. I guess his jeans have come off—a loud clonk and the rattle of coins brings an image of his denims meeting the wooden bench. Did keys in his pocket, a belt, or his wallet maybe make that noise?

Who will service him when I'm gone?

I don't care.

A melancholic fugue settles over me, and I forget for a few moments—forget everyone here, the attachments I've made, the day-to-day basics of my job. It doesn't feel so bad not thinking of them. Not when I have a new life ahead of me.

Questions form...ones I haven't entertained until now. Will I move into Ben's place or he into mine? Will we live apart for a while until we're doubly sure of where we're going? Will I take to being a plumber's mate?

I'll miss the camaraderie between the girls here. Miss seeing Shelley's smiling face when I clock in.

I shall miss Madam.

But I won't miss the men.

The curtain opening jerks me away from musing. I turn, one hand on the corner of the red leather bed, and face Mr Sanders. How I used to love the magnificence of him, the planes of his chest, the muscles from there to his abdomen, so chiselled, so...orgasm-inciting. Strong, hairless, football-player thighs. Shins greased with oil, the dim lighting accentuating the bones. Calves, their soft curve a lure to touch — instigating wicked thoughts of them resting on my shoulders, his rigidity in my mouth, balls in my hand. He inspired awe the way he can stand there without the slightest hint of embarrassment, his cock hard, ready.

Not anymore.

"My, my. What a special sight you are," I whisper, getting into role, hating myself for how easy it is. "Come to me." *One last time.* "Come lie on the bed and let me touch you all over. Every inch of you."

His dick bobs, and he clenches his hands into fists. His features darken — brows drawn to the bridge of his nose, eyes narrowed — but not in annoyance. Lust has driven his facial contortions, almost as though his erection pains him.

He moves towards me with the grace of a predatory jungle beast, muscles taut beneath the honey-hued skin, brown eyes trained on mine. A connection sparks, the one all humans experience when hormones take over, and a shimmer of desire escapes from my centre and wanders up my abdomen to my nipples. They peak, yearn for him to touch them with a lover's caress, not the hands I usually adore—hard and unforgiving.

I want Ben not him.

Have I become addicted to sex, or am I focused on having rough quickies so that I'm controlling my nymphomania and not the other way around?

I have no time to ponder. Mr Sanders and a brewing orgasm demand my attention. He climbs upon the bed with refined agility. He lays flat and slides one foot from the end of the bed, back. His leg flops outwards, his sole resting against the side of his other knee. Tight testicles, one slightly larger than the other, hang just enough to cover the lower crack of his arse. A smattering of hair either side of them tapers up into an abundant mass of black curls, his thick cock resting on top of them.

He links his hands behind his head—a pillow—and stares at me. His hooded, smoky gaze drinks me in. Two paces and I'm beside the bed, the fingertips of my left hand stroking the flesh of his flank, the fingertips of my right stroking my labia. Both hands move in the same direction at the same time, and I marvel that my cunt is so much softer than his skin.

I smile and sweep my hand across his stomach one more time then step to the steel table on my right. The top drawer of a filing cabinet beneath reveals silk scarves, ropes, and shoe laces. Black scarves gain my attention—their colour somehow fitting for my last day—and I pull four out and turn back to Mr Sanders.

He lifts his head to move his hands and spreads both legs, his heels and wrists now at each corner of the bed. I wrap a scarf around each and tie them to the metal leg poles of the bed, making loose knots. His cock strains in his eagerness for stimulation.

He can't touch himself or me, and is completely at my mercy. It's better like this. Less intimate.

I select a condom from a tub on the table and slip it beneath his back. "How do you want me?"

Please just ask for a hand job...

His eyelashes touch his cheeks, two blinks, and he smiles, a lazy lift of one corner of his mouth. "Sit on me. Face the door so I can see your arse. And get the whip."

A momentary flash of relief fills me. It will be more anonymous this way. I won't have to rub my nipples against his broad chest and hold his biceps, dig my nails into the flesh encasing them.

I get the whip and seat myself to his specification, arse on his stomach. His cock hot in my hand, I masturbate him, his foreskin ruched then taut, ruched then taut. He shifts, and his upper body judders.

"Ah...the wrist scarves... I need to touch your arse." His strained voice matches the rigidity of his dick.

"You know the rules, Mr Sexy. Rules you created. No touching on your part."

My pun nudges my lips into a smile, and his low rumble of laughter is quickly chased by a sharp exhalation.

"Do you like that? Like the way I touch your cock?"

He lifts his pelvis and digs his heels into the bed to keep balance. I rock my arse back and forth in time with my hand around his prick and imagine the strain on his neck as he cranes his head off the bed to watch. My cunt, slick from juices, glides against his stomach, and the scent of my sex wafts up.

"Can you smell me? Smell my cu—"

He lets rip a yell, hips bucking, cock pulsing, and pre-cum crowns the top of his dick. "Stop!"

"Stop?" I work faster, giving him a smart strike with the whip on his outer thigh. "*Stop*?"

"Yes! I can't...can't fucking..."

"Can't. Fucking. What?" I tighten my grip, gyrate against him, the friction a delicious rasp against my clit. Strike him again. "I'm not far from coming myself, Mr Sexy. And if I do this too often" —I lean forward and lick the head of his cock—"you'll come before me." Another lick, a suck, a strike. "Won't you?"

"Uh. Shit, untie me. I need to touch—"

"No!"

Still maintaining my rhythm on cock and clit, I reach behind me and retrieve the condom, ripping the packet open with my teeth. Sheathed, his girth renders the rubber tight. The condom's rim bites into the base of his cock. His breathing accelerates, and his chest heaves against my arse cheeks. More liquid moistens my labia, and I kneel, stare at the door, and hold his dick upright. Lowering onto him, I thrust down. He fills me fast. The tip bumps my cervix, the result a shot of painful pleasure along with the stretching of my hole. With a strict, hard rhythm, I throw the whip aside, imagine he's Ben and ride him—the fingers of one hand on a nipple, the fingers of the other thrumming my clit.

"Do you like this kind of ride? Like the way I feel around your cock?"

A *donk* indicates the back of his head has hit the bed, but he raises it again, his stomach muscles hard under my arse proof of that.

"Uh, yeah. Fuck, yeah. Harder. Go faster."

I comply. He splays his toes, digs his heels into the bed, lifting his arse to meet my downward plunges.

His calf muscles bulge with the effort of holding himself up. Just the sight of those toned beauties triggers a thrill in my stomach that reaches out to my clit with tendril fingers. Are Ben's like that? I ratchet downwards—hard—and lift slowly, repeating the action, chasing the imminent explosion.

"Mistress…Darkness. I, uh, I…"

"Come hard. Harder than you have before."

I'm going to come.

His yowl joins mine. I close my eyes, dig my nails into my breast, strum my bud faster, faster, the pressure building and crashing over me in undulating spasms. Goosebumps spring up on my skin, and I slow my movements on my clit, a pulsing bead beneath my fingertips. Still riding him, I open my eyes and count, waiting for his release.

It comes with a frantic buck of his hips and throttled vocals, his head once again meeting the bed. I judge him spent by the throb of his cock vein flickering slower and bring my rhythm to a stop. He lowers his arse and legs, resting like a panting star upon red leather.

I climb off him and the bed, note the angry red half moons on my breast, the dampness of my Brazilian, and the way he is, muscles relaxed, fingers curled from the fists he usually clenches. His eyes closed, he smiles then blows air through pursed lips.

I walk over to the sideboard and select another whip. Back at the table, I do what I've always done and strike him with it, telling him he's a filthy boy and I'm punishing him for coming here.

I'm sick of it. Sick to my stomach.

Unable to hit him any more, I throw the whip to the sideboard and take a moment to calm down. I'm angry at myself, at him, at the world.

"Same time next week?" he asks.

I turn to face him. He's opened his eyes, gaze seeking me.

"No." I begin untying the scarves from his ankles, the knots tighter from his frenetic movements.

"No?" He snaps his head up, eyes wide. "Have I...did I do something wrong?"

I move to his wrists. "No."

His cheeks redden, and his lips work, no sound slipping past them.

I can't look at him, so busy myself with the final knot.

"But...how will I find you? I'll visit wherever you go."

I risk a glance at him and wish I hadn't.

Another fish hooked, it seems.

"I won't be in this line of work anymore. I'm changing careers."

Released from his binds, he sits up, slides off the bed, and stands before me, cock limp, condom hanging. He clasps my shoulders, his strong hands too much.

I pull away.

"But...I can't imagine doing this kind of thing with anyone else," he says.

Me neither, but for different reasons. I can't imagine doing this with anyone but Ben from here on out.

I look into his eyes one last time. "Goodbye, Mr Sanders."

I walk away from him, head held high, into my dressing room.

It isn't until the door is closed and my back rests against it that I allow my bottom lip to fully quiver. A sob wrestles for liberation, and I swallow it down. I've done it.

I've serviced my last client.

* * * *

16th June – Afternoon

So, this is it. All clients sent away happy with my performance, unhappy that they were unaware until the final curtain that it would be their last with me. Madam saw me off with tears in her eyes. I'd like to think some of that moisture was genuine sadness at me leaving, but I'm not stupid enough to realise she's counting up the lack of money I would have earned her until she replaces me.

I must tell Shadow.

I need breathing space to untie the knots that began much like those around Mr Sanders' ankles and wrists. Over this past week mine have tightened to an unbearable degree, so tight that I wonder if I can ever work them loose. Leaving here is the only way to cut myself free.

I gathered my personal items together, then sat on my beanbag bed in the dressing room to write the final entry of my time in this dungeon. I wonder now — will my travels take me to a calmer place, where the wind doesn't blow sand into my eyes as I stand on my new beach of life? Will new experiences erase my past, or at least allow them to stay at the back of my mind? And, will those new experiences eclipse those that have gone before?

I hope so, but I must close this entry with the belief that Ben has the ability to loosen those knots.

Chapter Eighteen

Freedom

I'm standing in the middle of my living room, nervous as hell—unusual for me—because it's Friday, it's *the night*, and I've been worrying that I won't be everything Ben hopes for. It's a tall order, one I want to live up to so badly, but when emotions are involved, it makes everything so different, doesn't it?

Oh, I can whip with the best of them, cuff a man and strike him until his skin grows red and he's whimpering in pleasure-pain, but to do that to someone I care for, even though he wants it? I don't know.

I'm hoping desire will be my guide, that these thoughts will vanish once I see Ben naked, his cock hard and ready for me, his excitement infusing me and making mine heighten.

You can do this, Klara. It'll be okay. But there's something else you have to deal with first.

Shadow enters the room, all dressed up for a night on the town. Her hair shines from a recent wash and blow dry, and the dress she has on—dark green taffeta—is to die for. Maybe she'll let me borrow it someday.

She smiles at me, somewhat shyly, and I find that odd. We've always been so open with one another, always shared our dreams and desires, yet with special men in our lives now, it seems to have built a wall between us. Sad, that, but something I can knock down right now.

"I've met someone," I blurt. "I think I love him."

She stares at me, kholed eyes going wide, and a huge smile stretches her red lips, making her beautiful face even more lovely. "Oh, my God! I'm so pleased for you. Who is it? When did you meet him? Is it someone from work? Is it serious?"

I laugh at her barrage of questions and sit on the edge of the sofa, patting the seat next to me so she can sit there. My tight jeans chafe my clit, and my nipples perk beneath my T-shirt at just the thought of me telling her about Ben. God, I have it bad, don't I?

"Bloody hell, Ursula. One thing at a time!"

She perches beside me, putting her black leather handbag on the floor beside her feet, and I note the high heels on her dainty feet match the dress.

I want them.

She takes my hands in hers and rests her head on my shoulder. "I've wanted this for you as much as I've wanted it for myself. I need answers!"

So I tell her all about Ben, and she nods when I try to explain that it doesn't seem rational to fall in love with someone so quickly, to feel that you've been with them forever when you haven't. I knew she'd understand.

"I know exactly how you feel," she says, giving my hands a little squeeze. "So you'll understand why I've decided to move out, be with Luke at his place?" She lifts her head, looking me in the eye, and hope that I'll give my blessing burns there bright as day.

"Fuck, yes. Do it. We've waited so long for this kind of thing. When are you going?"

"We haven't decided yet. I wanted to tell you first before we made any decisions."

"What the hell has it got to do with me? Please, don't ever live your life based on someone else's opinion. It's for living—you've got to live it for yourself, for what *you* want, what makes *you* happy. Even if Ben wasn't on the scene I'd feel the same way. I thought you knew me well enough by now to at least know that." I smile so she doesn't take my words the wrong way, so she knows that I'm not annoyed with her.

Tears fill her eyes. "I love you, Klara, you know that?"

"I know it, and we're both going to live wonderful lives, you hear me? Go out with Luke tonight, make your plans. I know I'm going to when I go to Ben's in a bit."

* * * *

I've changed into a more seductive outfit. The jeans and top weren't making me feel...sexy, and I'll be honest and say, after seeing Shadow in her gorgeous dress, I felt a bit drab in comparison. My short, slinky black number does the trick. It gives me confidence, sends me into role and, along with my large gym bag filled with toys, I'm just about ready to head over to Ben's. I can't see us using all the toys in one night, but you never know. Stranger things have happened.

He texted me just now. *'Hurry up! I can't wait much longer, kitten!'*

I reply with *'I'm on my way!'*, slip my phone in my handbag and pick up my holdall. I leave my apartment and make my way down in the elevator, the journey seeming to take forever. It's funny to know I have kinky shit in the holdall, that no one knows what it contains except me. As I step out of the elevator and strut across the foyer to the main doors, I smile as the man behind the desk eyes me, probably wondering why I have such a big bag when I'm clearly dressed to go out on the pull or something. I reckon he knows what me and Ursula do for a living, yet he's never said anything—just looks at us in a knowing way. I've thought a couple of times what I'd do if he turned up at the dungeon, whether I'd fuck him or tell Madam it's a conflict of interest.

I giggle at that and throw out thoughts of him, instead thinking about Ben's reaction when he sees what's inside. It's all very well imagining, all very well thinking you'll like the slash of a whip or the crack of the cat-o-nine-tails, but when actually presented with them, sometimes bravado deserts you.

Will Ben embrace what I have to offer, or will he shirk away?

Of course, I'm hoping he'll embrace. Although I'd never had BDSM experience before working for Madam, I'd quickly come to enjoy it, and I'll miss it if Ben decides that kind of thing doesn't do it for him. Still, adding a little kink to spice things up doesn't mean we have to use toys, does it? We can be inventive in other ways.

At my car, I heft the holdall onto the back seat then climb into the front, starting the engine with a bubble of nerves popping in my belly. The nerves aren't as bad as they were earlier—they're more like excitement now—and I thank myself for changing my outfit. It's amazing what clothing does for you, isn't it?

The traffic is light considering it's a Friday night. I wonder if the hordes of people left for home early, many of them commuting to this sprawling city every day, or staying over for the week and returning home at weekends. I don't hit any red lights, don't follow any erratic or slow drivers that would hike up my annoyance level, and smile that hey, things really are going my way lately.

I arrive at Ben's and park up, wondering if he's watching for me out the window like I did the other night. I'd love it if he was. Collecting my bag then locking the car, I sashay towards his flat—just in case he *is* watching—swaying my hips, my black high heels striking the asphalt with a pleasing snap of sound. I'm getting more into role the closer to him I get.

He swings open his door, eyeing me up and down, a light pink flush on his cheeks. "Jesus fucking Christ, you're beautiful. I can't get over you. Can't get over the fact you're here—that we're here and it's Friday."

He takes the holdall from me, raising an eyebrow in silent question, and I tap the side of my nose.

"That's for the bedroom," I say.

"God, get in here right now!" He tugs me inside, closing the door loudly, and lets the bag go. It lands on the floor with a thud, tinkle and clatter. "What the hell have you got in there?"

I don't answer, just smile, waiting for him to make a move.

"Come here. For God's sake, come here," he grinds out.

I step into his arms, and the nerves disappear, a spread of comforting warmth replacing them. My cunt clenches, clit taking up its usual throb, and I wind my arms around his back and press myself to his chest. He kisses the top of my head, his hands running up and down my back, fingertips skating over the bare flesh where my dress stops just below my shoulder blades. The contact has me lifting my head and crushing my mouth to his, showing him with my lips and tongue how much I've longed for tonight, longed for him my whole adult life. He responds in kind, and a soul-searing kiss, the likes of which I've never experienced before, blows my mind.

I'm not going to last long before I climax.

I reluctantly break free and whisper against his mouth, "The bedroom."

He releases me, keeping eye contact, and lifts the holdall. It tinkles and rattles again. "I'm so not going to ask. Just let you show me."

He takes my hand, leading me towards his bedroom, and I'm shocked and so bloody pleased at what I see inside. Candles, so many of them, sit on a chest of pine drawers and light one corner of the room a warming cream, leaving the rest in sensual shadow. The flames flicker, and I narrow my eyes and fancy they look like a gorgeous open fire. They're scented—jasmine and vanilla, I'm guessing—adding to the romantic feel. He's taken the time to cover the bed in rose petals— red and a deep pink—and more roses are arranged beautifully in a black glass vase on the bedside table.

I want to cry.

"Oh, Ben…"

He drops the holdall beside the bed. "I thought it'd make a nice change for you. I mean, I imagine you don't get much of this in a dungeon."

"It's perfect." I look at him, a lump forming in my throat, tears stinging. "You're perfect."

He smiles, the one-corner-of-your-mouth-tilting-up kind, and stands there as though lost, like he doesn't quite know what to do next. He clenches and unclenches his hands, shifts from foot to foot. He needs direction, I see that, and, taking a deep breath, I become Mistress Darkness.

"Strip."

He widens his eyes, although a glint of devilishness shines from them. This is all new to him, a journey he hasn't taken before, and I welcome him as my passenger. I can tell he'll take to this well by the way he's removing his clothes, looking at me as he climbs onto the bed and lays in the middle on top of a cream quilt. With his arms by his sides, his cock growing, legs slightly apart, head propped up on two pillows, he is divine.

The perfect specimen.

And all mine.

I move to the foot of the bed and stare at his broad shoulders, loving the way they curve down to the muscled tops of his arms, and how the hairs on his forearms stop at the crook of his elbows. A light smattering of hairs cover his wrists, tapering to nothing on the backs of his hands, but those on his legs are thick all the way up from his ankles to the juncture of his thighs. The curls surrounding his cock...God, they call to me, make me want to bury my nose in them as I suck him off.

My clit throbs hard. I inhale a sharp breath. Studying him will get me off if I'm not careful, so I walk to the holdall and unzip it.

"Do you want a gentle introduction?" I ask. "I think that might be better."

"Whatever you want," he says, voice hoarse. "I'll take anything you want to give me, try anything once."

"Good." I bend over and sort through the toys, wondering what to select. I choose a brand new toy, a flogger, and although the leather strands are soft because it hasn't been used yet, it'll give him quite a bite. "Do you want me to be Mistress Shadow for tonight? Show you what I can do?"

"Yes, kitten, but the night is long, right? You can be Klara after…"

I nod, a curt bob of my head, and sigh deeply to get my mind in the right place. There is no room for sentiment, no room for me to think about hurting him.

"You must have a safeword. In case it gets too much. You might want me to stop." I pull out the flogger and lay it beside him on the bed so he fully understands what I'm saying.

He swallows, eyeing the toy. "Okay."

"Choose one," I say, purposely making my voice strident.

He looks from the flogger to me, his facial expression showing awe and a little shock at the same time. I suppose I *am* different now to what he's seen so far…but he asked for it!

"Jesus, you're fucking hot," he says, moving one hand towards his cock.

"Leave it!" I snap. "Don't you *dare* touch until I say so."

He eases his hand away and fists the quilt.

"Your safeword. What is it?" I take lube out of the bag, a condom, and a short, thin butt-plug. If he's never done anything like this before, a larger toy might put him off trying it again. I place them on the bed next to the flogger.

He looks at them, then up at me. "Oh, God. Um, I don't know. What kind do your clients use?"

"Anything. Pick anything, and hurry up about it!" I stand upright and jam my hands on my hips, staring at him, completely in my comfort zone now. *Thank God…*

"Um…uh, dove. Will that do?"

"It's fine, but you *must* use it when you can't take any more, understand?"

He nods, bites his bottom lip.

I remove my dress, not in the mood for anything seductive and fancy. Being slinky can come later. I want the shock of him seeing me quickly. I throw the garment to the floor, leaving my heels on, and he stares at me, exhaling a long, slow breath. My tits bounce as I walk to the foot of the bed and kneel on the end.

"Oh, my fucking God," he whispers, cock hardening further.

"Turn over but stay in the middle of the bed."

He complies, and I take a moment to admire the swell of his arse, the cleft at its centre, hairs helping to make it a dark and shadowy place. My cunt aches…my breasts, too.

"Open your legs then get up on your knees. Stick your arse out."

He does so, folding his arms then resting his forehead on them. His cleft is a little wider now, but I still can't see the pucker I so want to see. I shuffle up the bed, settling between his legs, and pick up the flogger. I tease him with it, ensuring the strands brush his arse cheeks softly, just so he knows I have the toy and will use it in an altogether different way very soon. He releases a low "*Mmm*" and juts his arse out some more, as though letting me know it's okay to proceed to the next step.

Without warning, I lift the flogger and bring the strands down on his arse, watching him jerk his hips towards the mattress in an instinctive move to get away from what caused him pain.

"Ah, fuck!"

"Did you like that, or should I stop?" I wanted to remind him he had a choice—some men new to this often forgot all about their safeword.

"Do it again," he says.

I smile and tease him a bit more, not wanting him to know when I'll strike next. When he relaxes his arse cheeks, when the dimple at the centre of each rounds out, I quickly lift the toy and bring the strands down—harder than last time.

He lifts his head, straightens his arms so he leans on his hands, dips his back, and lets out a strangled keen. His pose is so erotic, such a turn-on, that I fight the need to stop this game, turn him over, and plunge down onto his cock. Instead, I whip him again while he's still recovering.

"Oh, Jesus, that hurts. Oh, ah, fuck it!"

He flops flat on the bed, thumping the mattress with one fist while gripping a pillow corner in his other. One cheek rests on the bed, and he stares at the wavering candle flames, the light from them dancing over one side of his body. He breathes fast, and sweat breaks out on his temple, a drip of it meandering over his cheekbone.

His reaction and the sight of him like that has my cunt leaking.

"Enough?" I bark.

"Yes, for now."

"Back on your knees again."

He adopts the position, and I nestle close to his protruding arse, taking the lube from beside him. I unscrew the cap and squeeze a generous amount onto my fingers, then glide them up that beautiful, dark chasm, paying particular attention to his hole. He groans, the sound muffled by the quilt, and I massage him for a while, letting his mind get used to what I'm obviously going to do. He's seen the plug, he isn't stupid…but it's better that he becomes accustomed slowly.

After a few minutes of me stroking, I circle his hole and, on the fifth rotation, ease one finger inside. It's hot in there, his muscles clamping around my finger, and I gently ease in and out, stretching his rim. Once I'm satisfied he's sufficiently primed, I reach for the butt-plug. It's smooth, has flat stoppers either side of the base to prevent it getting sucked right up inside, and I run its tip between the top of his cleft to cover it in lube. As I draw it down his crevice, I withdraw my finger and replace it with the plug. I don't push it in and out but leave it there.

"Turn onto your back."

I can't give him an hour-long session. I'm burning with the heat of lust, teetering on the edge of a delicious orgasm. I can't wait any longer. I watch him roll over, see the tell-tale glisten of pre-cum sitting in his cock slit, and fuck—*yes!*—I've got him.

"I think that's enough games from Mistress Darkness for tonight. She's horny and wants your cock inside her. She can't wait—just like you."

I reach for the condom and tear the wrapper with my teeth. Discarding the refuse, I straddle him, arse resting on the tops of his thighs, and reach out to take his cock in one hand. He sucks in a breath, staring at me as though he adores everything about me, and I almost, almost give in and become Klara. I retain eye contact as I roll the condom down his length—a length that is just the right amount for me, the girth and head I'm sure will be a perfect fit for my cunt. He throbs, licks his lips, and lifts his hands then drops them again when I don't move forward into his embrace.

"You can fuck Klara later." I lift up, position his tip at my entrance, and stare at him.

"Please, just fuck me," he says, then groans.

I sink down, revel in the sensation of him filling me, that wonderful stretch I've been longing for since I met him. He doesn't disappoint—I could have his dick in my cunt all damn day. Unable to go into this slowly, I fuck him hard and fast, bracing myself with my hands on his chest. He reaches up between us and tweaks my nipples, twisting and pinching with just the right pressure. Pleasure radiates from my hard nubs, zipping straight down to my clit, where it burns and begins the swarm of sensation I crave.

"What's it like with that plug up your arse?" I ask. "Good, does it feel good?"

"It's...different."

My channel clenches around him, and he groans, long and loud, squeezing his eyes shut while raising his hips. I lean forward so his pelvis rubs against my clit, and those few strokes set my orgasm raging. I dig my nails into his chest, grit my teeth and fuck him harder, jamming down so forcefully his tip butts my cervix. The pleasure-pain of that is exquisite, and I ride it out, drowning in the way my orgasm crashes through me, plundering every part of my body.

"Ah, ah, fuck! Shit, I'm coming!" Ben rasps, pinching my nipples more harshly. "Fuck, you feel so good. So fucking hot and good."

I plunge down then up, repeating each downward thrust and quick, upward jerk until I feel his cock pulsate and hot fluid fill the condom. His hips spasm, and he forgets my nipples as cum spurts from him, his head thrashing from side to side. My arms and legs grow heavy, and sweat breaks out all over me, over Ben's chest. My hands slide, and I continue my assault on his cock until he moves his hands to my waist and makes me slow.

"Oh, God," he whispers.

He opens his eyes, stares at me with a glazed look, as though he's still coming down from the high. I smile and lean forward, brushing my lips over his, then snaking my tongue along his jawline and to his earlobe. I suck it into my mouth, swirl the tip of my tongue over it, then let it go.

With my mouth close to his ear, I ask, "Are you ready for Klara now?"

About the Author

Natalie Dae is a multi-published author in three pen names writing several genres. She lives with her husband, children, and three cats in an English village. She writes full time and is also a cover artist and blog designer. In another life she was an editor. Her other pen names are Sarah Masters and Charley Oweson.

Natalie Dae loves to hear from readers. You can find her contact information, website details and author profile page at http://www.total-e-bound.com

Total-E-Bound Publishing

www.total-e-bound.com

Take a look at our exciting range of literagasmic™
erotic romance titles and discover pure quality
at Total-E-Bound.